A CLEVER FOX

ALSO BY JULIA V. ASHLEY

SHORT STORY COLLECTION
Jazz by Faelight

FAIRIE MARKET MYSTERIES
A Charmed Moon
An Enchanted Heart
A Clever Fox

JULIA V. ASHLEY

A CLEVER FOX

A FAERIE MARKET MYSTERY
BOOK THREE

DREAMARC

The story, all names, characters, and incidents portrayed in this production are fictitious. No identification with actual persons (living or deceased), places, buildings, and products is intended or should be inferred.

A CLEVER FOX

DREAMARC Press
Madison, Mississippi
dreamarc.com

ISBN: 979-8-9892064-4-5 (hardback)
ISBN: 979-8-9892064-5-2 (paperback)
ISBN: 979-8-9892064-6-9 (ebook)

Book Art and Cover Design © 2025 DREAMARC Press

Cover Photography by Anivino, Maxborovkov, and Alex_Skp

First Edition: 2025

To Tohbi, my shadow to the end

And

To Lusawen, who left too soon

Chapter 1

WARWICK

Faelight pulsed in a sinister rhythm from within the Faerie Market. Slouching against a cracked plaster wall across the street, Warwick studied the barrier to the In Between, searching for an opening. The market's guard, an ill-tempered minotaur, patrolled its perimeter, barring access from the human city of New Orleans.

The minotaur stopped and snorted as if sensing Warwick's presence. It snuffled, trying to catch his scent, when a screech seized its attention. A wretched two-headed beast clawed its way through the market's barrier. A chimera, its goat head cloven in half and its lion's maw dripping blood. The guard herded the hideous creature back into the In Between, and the market winked out of existence until the next quarter moon.

"What hell has grown in my absence?" Warwick asked the empty street before him. Leaving the comfort of the century-old building, he went to look for clues as to what festered there.

As he crossed, humans converged on the market, and Warwick halted.

Stepping back onto the sidewalk, the goblin blended back into the shadows.

Chapter 2

SABINE

A dark figure drifted through the mists shrouding the river walk. It drew close, then dissipated before Sabine could make out its form. This near the river, creatures walked the space between New Orleans and the Beyond. In the pre-dawn hours, dense fog would blow in from the Mississippi River to hide them from view. Warm light from the lampposts fought against the heavy blanket but could not keep up. A cackle like the cry of seagulls sounded over the river.

Fearing the River Fae might be on the hunt, Sabine fell into the current of fog as it rolled across the railroad tracks and down the steps to fill Jackson Square. She pulled her auburn trench coat snug around her petite form, belted it tight, and listened for sounds of pursuit. The soft shushing of her slippers across the brick pavers blended with the sound of the river lapping against its stone banks. Otherwise, the fog was silent.

As the first light rouged the sky, New Orleans appeared as an unfinished watercolor. Its magenta and blues, its verde and violet bled together forming soft grays. Mornings like this, with the world muted, brought on a melancholy that suited Sabine, who had decisions to make.

Sabine was a witch who could not control magic. She possessed fox form but was no shifter. She was a thief bereft of the compulsion to steal. And she was a loner with an odd assortment of friends, all flirting with their own demons.

A treacherous fae had lured her housemate into the Beyond, and Meg had barely escaped. No thanks to Sabine.

Warwick, a gnarled goblin banished to the human world, had taken up residence in the small wooden shed behind her house and grumbled anytime Sabine came close.

A mite-infested crow named Bertrand had latched onto her, acting as her constant critic and sometimes conscience.

And a nasty black magic had implanted itself in her friend Detective Jean-Luc Thibodeaux. He'd always come to her rescue, but now that he needed her, she didn't know enough about magic to help him.

Sabine was angry at those who'd hurt her friends and angry at herself for not doing better, being smarter, more clever.

She slid through the fog, eddies swirling in her wake. The black iron fence enclosing Jackson Square materialized. Groggy crows inside cawed, cursing her for waking them. Sabine ignored their grumblings. She'd left her own grouchy feathered friend at home.

The laziest of crows, Bertrand, would sleep until Meg woke to hand feed him kernels of corn, as if he weren't a trash bird. He'd lived off of carrion and garbage before she adopted him. Or he adopted her. The distinction was still up for debate.

Ahead, the ghostly form of St. Louis Cathedral rose through the fog. Its old stones grumbled as its steeples caught the morning light. Sabine turned and drifted down Decatur. Along its length, street dwellers sheltered in doorways, positioned far enough apart for the illusion of safety from one another, while close enough to offer protection from anything else.

A black mutt lifted its head to watch her pass. Sabine whistled a low note, and its ears perked. Its tail wagged twice before it laid its head back on a young man's lap. Eyes still closed, the man laid a gaunt hand on the dog's neck, and the mutt gave a satisfied thump of its tail. In Latrobe Park, the homeless slumped together for warmth.

Looking up, Sabine realized her steps had once again led her to the French Market.

The open-air pavilion stood vacant. Its skeletal framework of racks stood empty. The glow from the line of streetlights ringing it cast an array of overlapping shadows around her feet. As Sabine drew near the pavilion, her multiple shadows merged into one, aimed straight at the market's center. She'd first noticed the odd drag on her shadow last fall in the Faerie Market. Now, its gravity extended to the human one as well. Sabine found herself unconsciously following it like a compass.

A low moan came from the structure, its shadows too dark, even at this hour. The sound was answered by another. Then another before it abruptly ceased, as if snuffed out.

The hair on her arms stood on end, yet Sabine still felt the market's pull. With an effort of will, she put her back to the pavilion. As she did, a figure with broad shoulders stepped from under the roof. Sabine remained motionless, letting the fog fall still around her.

Chin ducked, shoulders tense, Detective Jean-Luc Thibodeaux stepped from the market's shadows and into the light, moving as if against a gale wind. Once out, he stretched his neck, rolled his shoulders, and shook out his hands before disappearing up Barrack Street away from the market.

Falling into fox form, Sabine followed.

Chapter 3

THIBODEAUX

The French Market tightened its grip on Jean-Luc as he left. The clop of hooved feet followed. Jean-Luc's hand twitched toward his jacket, where his sidearm used to rest. He jammed the empty hand into his pocket and waited, hoping to find a horse-drawn carriage practicing its route before the tourists woke, but there was only a young man stumbling along as if waking from a drunken stupor or still in the grips of a drug haze. Strange that his steps sounded hauntingly like the clop of a horse.

As Jean-Luc turned the corner, the clop of hooves clattered to a stop. Black tendrils crept across his vision. Inhaling deeply, Jean-Luc clenched his fists and willed them down as if by physical force. They receded.

His shadow, stretching back to the market, grew taut until it broke and his silhouette fell into place against the wall to his left. Before him, golden lights blinked on in the corner coffee shop, and a server set small mason jars of flowers on a row of metal tables lining the sidewalk.

A shadow, joined his against the wall, low to the ground like that of a cat or dog. As soon as he spotted it, the shadow fell back out of view, and the familiar patter of padded paws followed close behind him. The muscles in Jean-Luc's chest loosened, and the shop door jingled as he entered.

A young man with cool brown skin and a bright smile greeted him from behind the counter. "What can I get you?"

"Coffee, black." Jean-Luc paused, then added, "Plus a latte and croissant, if you have one. I'll be outside."

The young man nodded. "Be right there."

Letting himself out a side door, Jean-Luc took a seat and stretched out his legs. Soon, an older woman with a motherly smile brought two mugs and a croissant, along with butter and two flavors of jam.

Jean-Luc took a drink of the black coffee, letting it scald his throat on the way down, as he leaned back in his chair. "You might as well have a seat before your coffee gets cold."

A shadow stretched up the wall, forming the silhouette of a petite woman. Sabine, the clever sneak thief who fancied herself an amateur sleuth, stalked past, her steps barely a patter against the sidewalk. She took the chair facing him.

With no greeting, Sabine grabbed the croissant, stuffed a third into her mouth, and spoke around it. "I'll pay for my own food, thank you."

Jean-Luc didn't comment. They both knew that was a lie, but he was satisfied she hadn't stolen it from right under his nose. Only because he'd already paid for it, though.

"What has you stalking me this early in the morning?" he asked, hoping it didn't involve any dead bodies, missing persons, or magic. Also, knowing it almost had to be one of those.

Sabine sipped her latte before asking, "What were you doing in the market before sunup?"

Evading the question, Jean-Luc finished his coffee and carefully set it on the table. "So, how are you and Ms. Armand settling into your aunt's house?"

Sabine finished off her croissant and countered. "Shouldn't you be headed to work by now?"

That stung. Jean-Luc set his mug down and contemplated just leaving. Conversations required a give and take, and Sabine the thief only knew how to take. Instead, he decided to come clean. "I'm on mandatory leave."

Sabine's eyes flared. "When you tore that float apart, you saved Meg and that pitiful Oliver, and whoever that witch's next victim would've been. Didn't that faux French witch confess? Meg said she did."

Jean-Luc waved off the server when she raised the carafe from inside, offering him another refill. "After the incident at the Mardi Gras parade, it was their only choice, short of firing me. And yes, Georgette gave a full confession. She claimed she used magic to trap three men, which caused one of their hearts to explode, and she admitted to ripping another heart out with those metallic nails of hers. But think about that for a minute."

Sabine sat back, arms crossed, mouth in a tight flat line, eyes scrunched. The server brought Jean-Luc a refill anyway, and he asked for a second croissant. When it arrived, he pushed the plate towards Sabine, who snatched it up and began tearing hunks off with her teeth, still thinking.

After a full two minutes, she grunted, and he nodded.

"That's right." Jean-Luc tested the second cup of coffee and was pleased that it was just as hot as the first. "The evidence was strong enough to put her away, but her lawyer will use her magical confession to get her moved to a psych ward where they'll probably let her loose within the year, two maybe."

Sabine grimaced, then gave him a narrow-eyed glare. "So, you didn't say, what *were* you doing at the market?"

Not ready to admit the market was calling to the dark thing living inside him, Jean-Luc turned the question back on her. "What were *you* doing there? No pockets to pick this early."

She wrinkled her nose. "I was thinking?"

"About?"

"Vengeance."

"Ah." Jean-Luc leaned back in his chair with his mug in hand. "Do you care to elaborate?"

"Should I tell a cop if I'm contemplating murder?" Her clever mouth curved into a wicked smile.

Jean-Luc matched it with one of his own. "According to the NOPD, I'm not a cop this morning."

Chapter 4

CARMICHAEL

The morning glow around the market grew, while the gloom inside remained the same. A miasma of black fog filled the pavilion's center. Carmichael, a newly promoted detective of the NOPD, took shallow breaths for fear of tarring her lungs with the black vapors. She hadn't noticed it while she laid in wait for her boss, Detective Jean-Luc Thibodeaux.

Twice, she'd tailed him, and twice he'd lost her. Determined to find out where he spent his time, she'd taken a wild shot and staked out a spot behind a stack of empty crates at the French Market and waited through the night. She'd studied his pattern. He left his apartment during the ungodly hours of morning to walk the streets. That, paired with his obsession with the increasing crime at the market, made it a reasonable guess.

And there he was. He'd taught her well

She'd parked several blocks away. The cold, damp fog had made for a miserable walk, but Thibodeaux was observant. He'd recognize her car, even in this fog. Sure, she could've asked him what he'd been up to, but then he might ask her the same question, and she wasn't prepared to answer.

Thibodeaux was practical to a fault. He wouldn't understand that there were other forces out there, forces practical folk refused to see. Powers too big to ignore. Once

Carmichael had discovered that something more powerful than the NOPD lurked in New Orleans, she wanted in on it.

The detective came, walked a circuit through the center of the market, then left, and Carmichael emerged from her hideout. Dawn slowly broke. The sun rose. Yet the area at the center of the pavilion remained murky. Carmichael tried to follow the detective, but found herself walking in a circle instead. The same circle that Thibodeaux had walked. She'd step forward and end up buffeted to the side.

"You, my pet, cannot simply walk into the heart of the market and leave at will," an incorporeal voice spoke out of the dark mist.

Carmichael searched the area. She was alone here at the center. "Who is that?"

"You know me," the voice said, sending an icy chill down Carmichael's spine that had nothing to do with the cool air. "We worked together once before, and I found you quite useful."

No. Please, no. Carmichael prayed.

Last fall, that cold voice had asked her to cover up a suspicious death. The young man, reported missing by friends, had been very much dead when Carmichael found him. His body swapped for that of a female murder victim. Carmichael was the only one, as far as she knew, who had seen the man's body, its chest blown open, ribs broken. Heart missing.

She blanched at the memory.

After that *favor*, Carmichael had risen fast through the ranks of the New Orleans Police Department. The voice had assured her she would. Carmichael wanted to give the credit to her hard work and Thibodeaux's encouragement. But she'd cut corners, changed records, and Thibodeaux had not been party to that.

Now, she was promoted to detective. She would not let this voice order her around. She would face it. Learn who wielded it and how to use them for her own purposes. She might have had some supernatural help to get to this position, but she'd paid for it.

As she tested the perimeter of her confinement inside the black mist, she watched for any sign of the man with the mysterious voice. On her second circle, she caught a figure in her peripheral vision, a tall man in the middle of the black haze, watching her. She'd not seen him approach. Hadn't heard him. As if he had coalesced from the mist.

The man towered over her. His features grew more distinct. He took a deep breath through his nose, and a sharp smile spread across his angular face, so pale that it looked almost blue.

Could he smell the fear wafting off of her?

Clearing her throat, Carmichael asked, "What have you come to offer this time?"

The tall man laughed. "I offer you a way out, unless you would prefer to remain here watching both worlds pass by. You do seem to enjoy your voyeurism."

Trucks pulled up and people of multiple nationalities tumbled out. They unloaded wares, setting up their tables and booths. A woman with a severe face and slight limp walked past Carmichael and the pale man without seeming to notice them.

"You there," Carmichael called out to her. She didn't respond. Carmichael spoke louder, using her official cop voice. "NOPD. I have questions about crimes reported here over the past few weeks."

The woman gave her no notice as she walked to the far side of the pavilion, her face lit by the rising sun. Carmichael took a breath to call out again when a vibration ran up her arm as a heavily tattooed man brushed past her. She reached out for him, but her hand passed through his arm.

"A perfect vantage point to see and not be seen. Yes?" the tall, pale man said.

"Let me out of this black funk of yours and then we'll talk."

"That would not work in my favor. Would it?"

"I won't agree to anything while trapped."

"As you say." The man stepped free of the mists and disappeared. He was simply gone. All but his voice. "We'll talk again in a few days. Or moons. However your people count time."

Carmichael fought to get past the barrier, her heart rapping against her ribs. "Wait. Before you go. At least tell me what it is you want. So, I'll be prepared to negotiate." There, that was a smooth response. She didn't agree to anything. Just that she would think on it.

His answer, if he was even there, was silence.

A short man with grizzled gray hair appeared through the mist next to her. Vendors walked past them both without noticing. The man wore a crimson hat, its color dulled by the mists, and wielded a long staff ending in a wicked hook. He jerked it free from a tangle of cloth at his feet. A tortured man, prone on the ground, groaned in agony.

Carmichael's mouth went dry and sweat slid down her temple. She licked her lips and drew her firearm. "Sir, lay down your weapon and step back. Hands in the air."

The red capped man looked about him as if he'd heard her but couldn't find her. His eyes glowed red as if lit from within.

His fingers, clutching the staff, ended in talons. He grunted and bent over the form on the ground.

The vendors went about their business of setting up for the day, unaware.

Carmichael trained her pistol on the man and raised her voice. "Sir, step back."

Instead, the grizzled man ripped at the body, spraying chunks of flesh and blood. The prone figure rolled onto its side. Its face turned her way, gouged with claw marks. The grizzled man took another swipe, spraying gore across Carmichael.

She fired. Three rounds. None met their mark.

The man's red eyes swung her way.

A scream welled inside her chest, and Carmichael dropped into a crouch to hold it in. Remain calm. The pale one won't let you die. She assured herself. Not if he needs your help.

Had the missing man from last fall been trapped like her? Was he encased in black smoke, seeing without being seen? When Carmichael had revisited his apartment, the walls had been stained amber with dried blood. Would that be her fate?

"My pet, do not be afraid." The tall, pale man stood next to her again, patting her head like a dog. "The redcap before you remains in the Faerie Market, outside of this place. Leave him to his business. He is quite thorough and will be done soon. Although he did let one get away earlier. You might have to clean that one up."

Carmichael stood, shaking off his hand. "You want me to clean up your mess?"

Her voice shook. She would do it. She knew she would, in the end.

"Not my mess. His." The tall man gestured to the grizzled one in the red hat, ripping away at his victim with bloody talons. "And soon it shall be yours if you choose to return to your world."

As the pale man next to her spoke, the grizzled one removed his hat, dipped it in the blood, and put it back on.

Bile rose in Carmichael's throat.

"What is it you want?" she asked, her voice raspy and sharp in her throat.

"One simple task to start. Remove the witch."

"Georgette? She's in jail," Carmichael said, watching the grizzled man stand and walk out of existence. His victim disappeared in the same moment.

"Not Mlle. Georgette. I will deal with her myself. I mean the foxy one who scampers about with no magic of her own, making a nuisance of herself."

Carmichael took a shaky breath and replayed the request. Then a nasty laugh bubbled up her raw throat. The pale man's brows rose.

"Would you like her locked up or dead?" she asked.

An equally nasty smile crossed his face. "Your choice, my pet."

Carmichael straightened her shoulders and cleared the bile from her throat. "My name is Carmichael."

His eyes lit as if bemused by her newfound boldness. "Very well. You may call me Baylur."

With that, he was gone and the toxic mists with him. Vendors startled to find her suddenly standing in their midst, sprayed with blood. Some shied away. Others pretended not to see her. One leered.

"Did I hear correctly? Your name is Carmichael?" asked a man with beetle-black eyes and a sharp face framed by grizzled gray hair. He lifted a blood-red fedora and tipped it in greeting. "Pleased to make your acquaintance."

Carmichael's blood ran cold.

Chapter 5

MEGAN

The morning fog dissipated as the sun rose over the roof, leaving a few stray ghostly wisps of mist under the two sparse oaks behind the cozy cottage. It would officially be Sabine's house once her aunt's will went through probate, and the petty thief threatened to charge Meg rent for her room. Meg ignored her, assuming it was all bluster, but you couldn't know for sure with that little witch.

Bertrand, the Magnificent Crow, sat on the scarecrow Sabine had erected in the middle of the small backyard to remind him he wasn't welcome. The wise Bertrand adorned it with shiny, found objects and used it as a post on which to preen his glossy black feathers. His trove of Mardi Gras beads, lost jewelry, and tarnished coins glittered in the fresh sunlight.

"Good morning, handsome." Meg stroked the tuft of feathers between his eyes before hitting 'Accept' on her phone. She'd come out here for privacy. Sabine wasn't home, but she might slip in at any moment, and Meg didn't want her overhearing her conversation. In the yard, she could keep watch to see if the wily witch appeared in her fox form.

Meg listened to the recorded message and took a deep breath. "I'll accept the call," she said. As she waited for the NOPD to connect her, a grumble came from the woodshed, telling her the resident goblin did not appreciate her taking the call outside. The line switched over to a croaking voice. Bertrand twisted his head to listen. It sounded very much like crow talk. Maybe it was. Then the voice shifted to the French accent of Meg's former employer, the witch Mlle. Georgette.

"Is this the tall one?" Georgette asked, having never bothered to remember Meg's name.

"This is Megan Armand. How did you get my number?"

The elegant witch had been locked up in the Orleans Parish Prison, leaving Meg unemployed. If she hadn't moved in with Sabine, she'd be out of cash by now.

"You shall get me out of this place," the witch demanded.

"That's not going to happen, Georgette. You killed people."

"Tch." The witch dismissed the comment. "You know the fae. You do what they will. Baylur took my heart, so I must take another. You do not want a heartless Georgette, do you? Be quiet and listen to my instructions. Go to the Sassy Witch's shop. You shall care for it while I am indisposed. But first, you shall go upstairs to my boudoir, find the enameled box under my bed, and guard it carefully. I will tell you when to bring it to me."

"I'm not getting you something to help you break out. They don't let you just walk into jail carrying enameled boxes."

The shed shook. Meg and Bertrand watched warily.

"I tell you to hush and listen, yet you yap and yap. Did you learn that from the little dog woman you live with?"

"How do you know I live with Sabine?"

"Mlle. Georgette knows."

Well, that was not illuminating at all. Dealing with Georgette had to mean trouble, but Meg's curiosity was piqued.

The crow *tocked*, and she nodded as she spoke, attempting to understand what sort of crime Georgette was conspiring.

"How do you expect me to get into your locked shop unless you want me to take Sabine to break in?"

"The fox woman is too clever for her own good. Do not take her. She will steal—"

A voice broke in. "One minute remaining."

Georgette gave a "Tch," to the recording and went back to giving out instructions. "You understand? That little yap dog pretending to be a witch is a thief. Do not let her in. The doors are warded, not locked. I am not a simple human with need of a lock."

"I've seen your wards. I'm not getting zapped."

Warwick, the goblin, threw open the shed and stood menacingly in the doorway. Meg couldn't tell if the gnarled man was scowling at her or if that was just his resting goblin face. "You shall not deal with that witch."

Georgette either didn't hear him, or ignored it. "You are so *stupide,* just like *le bébé sorcière.* The wards are not set for you. Do not be simple, Meg. Go, find the box, do not let the thief inside, and take care of the shop until I call you again."

Bertrand squawked and fluttered his wings.

Warwick squinted, grumbled, and leaned forward to make his way across the yard to the porch as if fighting under storm winds.

Meg had more important issues than grumpy goblins and squawking crows. "I'm not working in your shop for free. I have bills to pay."

"*Stupide, stupide.* Money is in the box under the settee. It is too full. It overflows. Take it. But do not let that little thief get her hands on—"

The recording cut her off. "30 seconds remaining."

"I refuse to let you deal with that witch, tall one." Warwick snarled, climbing the steps to the back porch.

"You stretched out, stilt woman, is that a goblin I hear?"

"Cr-r-rack," Bertrand chimed in.

"My name is not tall one or stretch or stilt woman. It's—" *Click.* The line went dead.

"Meg," Meg said to the empty line.

Warwick made a guttural comment about stretched humans and wayward witches as he let himself into the back door of Sabine's house. Bertrand *shrieked* and flew through the opening before the screen door slammed shut.

"She did offer me money," Meg announced to the empty backyard.

"Who's that?" Sabine asked, coming over the back fence in human form, because *of course she did*.

"Who are you talking to?" Detective Thibodeaux asked as he rounded the corner of the house.

Startled, Meg turned to answer him, but saw he was talking to Sabine. So, he'd been expecting her to come over the fence when he entered the yard. Because, *of course he did*.

"Are you two collaborating again?"

"Yes," they both said at once, agreeing for the first time since Meg had met the two of them.

"I'm going to need a drink to handle this, aren't I?" Without waiting for an answer, Meg followed Warwick inside and headed for the fridge to see if they had enough orange juice for mimosas, because it just wasn't appropriate to have straight bourbon before noon.

Chapter 6

WARWICK

Light flowed through the kitchen windows like a weak soup. Avocado-green cabinets hung along startlingly yellow walls. A long wooden table with a floral plastic cover sat in the middle of the room with a rack of pots and pans hung overhead. Despite his efforts to resist, Warwick begrudgingly found comfort in the witchling's home. This morning, he sought additional comfort in the sweet cream kept in her icebox. If only the blasted sunlight did not cut the room in half, he could reach it more comfortably.

The tall one passed in front of the window, blocking the sun long enough that he might pass unscathed. She popped a bottle of bubbly booze and added juiced oranges while he checked the icebox for frozen sweetened cream and settled himself at the table with a ladle.

"Warwick, use a spoon and bowl." Megan Armand, the tall one, took the cream from him, scooped out an insufficient amount, and set the bowl in front of him with a child-size spoon, and returned the cream to the icebox. "I'd offer you a mimosa, but it wouldn't go well with mint-chocolate chip ice cream."

Thibodeaux waved off Megan's offer of bubbles or cream and headed to the pot containing the bitter bean juice, but the slow drip of the kitchen faucet sidetracked the detective. Retrieving a wrench from the left kitchen drawer, he tightened the fixture, returned the tool, and poured himself coffee.

Nearly a moon span had passed since Warwick had moved here with Bertrand the Magnificent Crow, Megan Armand, and the witchling, Warwick being the most dignified of the quartet. In that time, he had never seen the detective here. Yet he seemed quite relaxed in the witchling's home.

Megan poured seed corn onto a saucer for the crow while the witchling glared from the doorway.

"Don't mind me. Just make yourself at home in *my* house."

Megan and Thibodeaux ignored the witchling's sarcasm while Bertrand muttered, "*It was mine first.*"

Warwick would like to hear the crow's tale at some point.

Sabine, the petite thief and incompetent witchling, snatched Megan's glass and climbed onto a stool at the end of the table. The ever-patient Megan Armand poured herself another without comment and leaned back against the counter. The detective positioned himself across from Warwick.

"Haven't you had enough caffeine for one morning?" Sabine asked.

Megan waggled her eyebrows. Warwick had learned this implied amorous desire. "You two've been on a coffee date this morning? Did you bring back beignets?"

"We were not on a date," Sabine said.

"She ate them all," Thibodeaux responded, smiling into his cup.

Odd how these creatures amused themselves with the most witless of comments.

Sabine downed her drink and held the glass for Megan to refill. "They were croissants, not beignets."

"So it *was* a date." Megan poured another concoction for her demanding little housemate.

Warwick had had enough of this useless banter.

"It never stops," Bertrand *tocked*, sharing Warwick's unspoken sentiment.

"Tall one, should you not tell the witchling about the deal you struck with the witch Georgette?"

All eyes snapped to her, and Megan choked on her drink. After a lengthy coughing fit in which the humans waited, eyes narrowed, Megan spoke. "I didn't make a deal. She wants me to reopen the Sassy Witch while she's *indisposed*, but I didn't agree to it."

"*Creekee,*" Bertrand prolonged the sound with several ululations.

"She offered you money, and you caved?" Sabine accused. It was quite interesting that the Magnificent Crow allowed the witchling to interpret his speech. Fascinating that he would demean himself so.

"No," Megan blurted out, glaring at the bird.

"*Creeeek.*" Which roughly translated to "Bullshit" in human speech.

"I mean," Megan fumbled. "I thought about it, but we got cut off."

"She called from jail?" Thibodeaux asked calmly. Too calmly.

"Yes."

"You gave her your number?" The witchling was getting feisty.

"No. At least I don't think I did. I don't know how you witches do your thing." Megan became sullen, most unattractive. "What were you two conspiring on your coffee date?"

Sabine finished her glass in one long swallow. "Still not a date."

"Revenge," Thibodeaux said, refilling his mug.

Sabine held out her glass. "If you're going to share our plans, I prefer the term 'vengeance' to 'revenge.'"

These humans required more fluids than any other creature Warwick knew.

"It's revenge for me," Thibodeaux said. The rapid-fire conversation ceased at the uncharacteristically hostile comment from the detective. The noble Thibodeaux explained. "That witch and her blue fae friend hurt *my* people in *my* city. It's personal."

"Call it what you like," Sabine said, without sounding like she meant it. "As long as we take the two of them out."

Megan startled at the venom in Sabine's voice. "Not like kill them, right? Because *we* don't *kill* people." She said this as if she thought the two of them might need a reminder.

The foxy woman gave her housemate a feral smile. "Whatever it takes."

Warwick shook his head at their ignorance. "You believe that you can take out the witch with your meager magic? Or even save your own hide against the fae? Mlle. Georgette is correct. You are a simple people. With simple notions."

The crow croaked, *"They try, bless their hearts."*

Sabine narrowed her eyes at the bird.

Warwick contemplated his empty bowl before speaking further. "You should each concentrate on your own darkness and leave matters of magic to those who understand them."

Thibodeaux carefully set his cup down and folded his hands. Malice wafted off of him. "You think I should let the witch loose to menace the city again? And that fae doesn't need to answer for his crimes?"

Bertrand *creaked,* followed by a long a slow *rattle,* and the goblin nodded in agreement.

"The Magnificent Crow sees it." Must Warwick spell everything out? "The dark heart of the Faerie Market has been calling." He made eye contact with the witchling, the detective, and then the tall one. "And each of you has answered."

They looked suspiciously at one another. When they turned their attention back to him, Warwick met their glares until each turned aside. All but Thibodeaux.

The detective let the goblin see the tendrils of dark magic slither across the whites of his eyes, staining his irises. Like a parasite, it grew inside him. Warwick didn't know how much control it had over the detective. The man's sharp mind still had its edge, but which of them controlled the blade?

Bertrand *tocked,* twisting his head to examine each of them with his beady black eyes.

Megan ducked her head and hummed to herself.

Sabine grunted.

Thibodeaux remained deadly silent.

Warwick nodded. He had their attention. "It will take you if it can. You must not give it the chance. Henceforth, none of you is to go near the market, human or otherwise."

Megan picked at her nails. "No problem. What does the French Market have that any of us need?"

"Will you be too busy aiding and abetting the witch felon to hunt for your abusive fae-friend at the market?" Sabine asked. Warwick expected sarcasm from the petite witchling but not her bitterness.

"I didn't say I'd help her."

"You didn't say you wouldn't either."

Thibodeaux's brow furrowed.

"*Caw. Caw. Caw.*" Bertrand flew in a tight circle around the room, startling the two women into silence. He landed and spoke in a rusty voice. "*The market. The market. The market.*"

Warwick placed his hands flat on the table. "Bertrand is right. Leave the witch alone. You are no match, and she is of little consequence compared to the rotting heart at the core of the Faerie Market. It burst through once. It may do so again. If it does, I do not believe it will heal itself as before."

"How do you propose we eliminate this 'dark heart' problem?" asked Thibodeaux in a cool, calculating voice. He took a slow sip of coffee, watching Warwick over the edge of his mug.

"No more dead hearts." Megan groaned.

"No *human* ones," the goblin assured her. Unless it becomes necessary, he thought. "You stay clear. I shall gather what information I am able."

A vein throbbed in Thibodeaux's temple. Bertrand's feathers puffed. Megan went silent. But Sabine exploded.

Flying off her stool, she jabbed a finger at Warwick. "The Faerie Market pulled you in and spit you out. Are you planning on crawling back in?"

"Are *you*?" Warwick asked calmly.

Her face flamed red.

Although these simple people readily exposed their emotions, he could not tell how much of her maelstrom was fear and how much was anger.

"No, she's not. None of us are. It's too dangerous," Megan announced, rising to her full height to loom over the table.

Sabine threw her hand in the air in dismissal and paced the length of the kitchen.

Megan pulled the cream from the icebox once more and filled bowls for everyone without asking. Possibly in hopes of cooling her companions' tempers. Warwick took his. Sabine waved hers away. Warwick relieved her of it. Megan absentmindedly set her own bowl in front of the crow, who twisted his head one way, then the other as if confused. Warwick graciously took the bird's bowl, too.

Thibodeaux accepted one, but set it aside. "Georgette is confined for the time being. But I can't risk that fae coming back through the market." The detective cocked an eyebrow at Sabine.

"Haven't seen the bastard since the parade," Sabine confirmed as she stalked the perimeter of the kitchen.

"You've been watching me?" Megan asked, reaching for her bowl, which was no longer there. She looked down in confusion.

"I've been watching for *him*." Sabine bobbled her head. The gesture's meaning was unclear to the goblin.

Megan stepped into the witchling's path. "I am an adult. I can make my own choices."

"You know the fae. You do what they will," Warwick parroted Georgette's words. That earned him a wounded look from Megan. Did she think he hadn't heard the whole conversation and knew how much she had left out?

Sabine rose on her toes and pointed a finger into the tall one's face. "I was there when you returned from the Beyond. I saw the bandages. Don't tell me you asked for *that*."

The two women glared at one another. Warwick knew this look—two combatants readying for battle.

"Arguing doesn't change the past nor help the future." The detective's words broke them apart. As they turned their backs to one another, their fierce expressions melted into pain and fear. Such odd creatures.

Thibodeaux rinsed his coffee mug, and the goblin snatched the detective's bowl of ice cream. Good, perhaps Warwick could keep the humans safely clear of the market while he figured out how to get back inside.

That hope was dashed as the detective turned to address the room.

"It's settled." Thibodeaux assumed the tone of a commanding officer. "Warwick and I will tend to the market. He can gather information, while I keep watch for Baylur. Megan, you stay put until we know that it's safe and let me know if Georgette calls again. Sabine, Warwick is right. Before anything else, you need training in how to use magic. Choose a sane witch to teach you this time."

Sabine abruptly stopped her circling. "Oh, you didn't just do that, did you? You didn't just tell the ladies to go off and amuse themselves while the guys do the dangerous stuff. Tell me you didn't."

"But I did," Thibodeaux said, and Warwick felt the darkness rising in the man, but he clenched his jaw and it seemed to clear.

"Sure, you go sniff around the market, because you don't already have *enough* of its darkness crawling around inside you? Warwick deals with a bunch of vendors selling cursed goods, because he *was one*? We all leave Meg alone because she's what? *Invulnerable* to that sadistic fae? And I'm supposed to go to kindergarten to learn my Abracadabras."

"So, you do understand the plan." Storm clouds covered the whites of Thibodeaux's eyes.

"Yep. I got it. Great plan! Hope y'all survive it." The witchling jerked the back door open. "See you later." She fell into fox form and shot across the yard and over the fence.

Warwick pushed the empty bowls aside. "She's rather volatile, is she not?"

Bertrand *creaked, "He should not have provoked her,"* and shot out after Sabine.

Thibodeaux touched Megan lightly on the shoulder. "Sabine has a point. Be careful."

"You watch out for your demons, and I'll watch out for mine." The tall one shrugged his hand off and disappeared down the hall, headed to the front of the house. "Lock up when you leave," she shouted over her shoulder.

Thibodeaux pinched the bridge of his nose and groaned.

"Splendid job taking charge, detective. I am sure we all appreciate it." Warwick tapped the table with his knuckles and left.

Chapter 7

SABINE

Dark clouds hung heavy in the midday sky, threatening rain. In fox form, Sabine skulked along the railroad tracks paralleling the French Market. A crow's shadow circled her on the pavement. She ignored the pestilent Bertrand, who'd better not report back to Thibodeaux. Passing Café Du Monde, she considered stealing a beignet, but even a half cup of powdered sugar per pastry couldn't lighten her mood.

A week had passed since the meeting in her kitchen, and Sabine's hide still rankled when she thought about it. Thibodeaux had agreed to her plan to go after the icy fae Baylur and the faux French witch Georgette. The two of them could take care of those fiends for good. Then that goblin comes into her kitchen, eats her food, and insists the market's a bigger deal, and just like that, Sabine's vengeance plan got sidelined. Suddenly, Thibodeaux goes from a team player to director of forces, if you could call their motley crew a force.

All save for Sabine. He expected her to go somewhere safe to learn the ABCs of magic. As if *he* knew anything about witchcraft. She could already cast spells. She'd done it, saving all their asses.

Regularly prowling the market, Sabine avoided the detective's notice as she surveilled the area. It didn't help that

Warwick might've been right. Although New Orleans was not generally dangerous to tourists if they weren't stupid, in the last few months, things had changed.

The French Market was still as busy as ever, but with a sketchier crowd. Not locals, but not tourists either. People who came looking for trouble found it at the market. Cops were on duty full time covering the increased activity. Drugs. Thefts—not her polite pickpocket type, but the down and dirty kind. A knifing here and there, plus one shooting. It was no longer the cheery, overpriced, kitschy place everyone knew and loved.

Sabine spotted Thibodeaux. He stalked the sidewalk alongside the French Market, surveying its booths of brightly colored dresses, scarves, Mardi Gras masks, tables of jewelry, and stands of art. She crouched down as he scanned the area, then disappeared, merging with the swarms of people flowing into the pavilion.

Just beyond the perimeter booths, darkness hung in the air, too dark to be mere shadows. A week had passed. The Faerie Market would be back tonight. A dangerous time for Thibodeaux to be here. Smokey black tendrils wormed their way out of the pavilion, reaching for her.

Stay back, she warned herself. Don't let it take you too. But Thibodeaux was in there. Who knew what trouble he'd get into without her?

As Sabine argued with herself, a disturbance started up towards the center of the market just beyond her sight. Coarse voices rose in an argument. Booths rocked and tables were jostled in a ripple that extended to the edge of the pavilion. Confused crowds stumbled out onto the sidewalks.

That's it. She was going in. Magic or no, she'd save Thibodeaux from himself.

Bertrand *croaked* a warning.

Ignoring it, Sabine crouched on her haunches, gave a ready wriggle to center herself, and leapt.

A hand caught the ruff of her neck and snatched her from the air. Stunned, Sabine dangled from wiry fingers. A regal woman of color drew her up until their eyes met.

"Not today, little fox. Not when the dark is calling." The woman tucked her firmly under one arm and sauntered down Decatur Street, head held high. She waved a hand at the screeching crow. He fell instantly silent and veered away. People parted in front of her. All differential, as if she were a queen. No one seemed to notice she carried a fox.

No matter how Sabine rabbit-kicked with her back feet, nipped with her snout, or writhed, the woman did not let loose. She had a grip of iron and a will to match. They traveled like this, walking slow and steady, leaving the French Quarter behind and entering the Tremé, the historical black sector of town. They moved down one block and up another until they reached a cottage painted robin's egg blue with a wide front porch and crystal clear windows shaded by lace curtains.

"You can wriggle all you like," the woman said with a heavy Creole accent. "I raised five young'uns, and they had three each. One thing I know how to do is keep a grip on an errant child." She marched up the porch steps just as the rain started.

Inside, the cottage smelled of nutmeg and sage. When they reached the kitchen, Sabine thought the woman would at last let her loose. She was almost right. The woman opened a broom closet, stuffed Sabine's fox form inside, and shut the door.

Immediately transforming, Sabine snatched for the knob to let herself out. Only, it didn't move. She twisted and rattled and banged, to no effect. She shouted and cursed and kicked the hardwood door, but it didn't budge.

The woman might be deaf. Or she might be just as stubborn as Sabine and not overly worried about the damage done to her door. Although it didn't look like Sabine had made a mark on the aged wood. She dropped back into fox form and began scraping the inside with her claws, hoping that the threat of shredding the door's finish would trigger the woman to open it. It didn't, and the door remained unmarred.

After an hour or more, alternating between cursing and throwing herself against the door in human form, barking and scratching the door while in fox form, Sabine curled up in the back corner to wait. Apparently, this woman had a plan for her, or she would've rung her neck while she had Sabine in her grip.

Where was that flea-bitten crow? Couldn't he help?

Alternately filled with rage and concern, Sabine continued cursing and scratching and barking, interspersed with fretful naps. She didn't know if she'd been sealed away for good. She comforted herself with the certainty that Bertrand would alert Thibodeaux, or Meg, or even Warwick.

If he hadn't abandoned her. Again.

Chapter 8

THIBODEAUX

Even without his badge and sidearm, Detective Jean-Luc Thibodeaux knew his presence still carried authority. He came to the French Market to gather information about its rotting core and to watch for Baylur. After the incident at the parade that might inevitably cost him the only job he'd ever wanted, Jean-Luc could no longer deny the existence of magic. He wished he could.

Since the meeting in Sabine's kitchen, Jean-Luc patrolled the market daily. At least now you have an excuse, he told himself. He shoved the thought away. The storm clouds that had been building all afternoon let loose, and he ducked under the pavilion.

He'd gained control over the darkness snaking its way through his consciousness. It rarely clouded his vision, except in the late hours of the night when he couldn't sleep. Or when he considered the ugly plan he and Sabine had contrived to do away with the double threat of Georgette and the fae. Or when he remembered his hands closing around Sabine's throat on the parade float.

Tendrils crept into his vision. He clenched his jaws and fisted his hands, and the darkness receded. He had control. Mostly.

At the market, Jean-Luc couldn't point to any specific vendor or customer and say, "There. That's the problem. That's the change, the darkening, the trouble-makers." But the market had a sinister disposition that grew heavier toward the center. Plastic masks leered. Portraits sneered, and the vendors wore equally intimidating faces.

A *squawk* interrupted his surveillance of the market's perimeter. Bertrand. Jean-Luc searched the bustling French Market for Sabine's familiar. Two crows fought over a crust of pizza smashed flat beside the metal garbage can just outside the food vendor area. Neither was Bertrand. The surrounding tables were clear of birds as the rain drummed against the metal roof. There, Bertrand clung to the side of a steel column.

Odd that Jean-Luc could tell his call apart from other crows, yet he still had no idea what the bird said. He wasn't entirely convinced that Sabine and the goblin knew either. More likely, they just projected their thoughts onto the bird, like Megan did.

Even more odd was the fact that the bird was squawking at him instead of at Sabine. Jean-Luc made a quick survey of the area beneath the vendor's tables for any sign of the fox. Sabine thought she was too clever to be spotted. And she usually was. Jean-Luc probably missed spotting her more times than he caught sight of her. And chances were, the times he did see her were only because she decided to let him.

Bertrand stretched his wings and *croaked* a desperate message that Jean-Luc couldn't decipher.

"I'm sure Sabine's up to no good. What would you have me do about it?" he asked the crow. It *tocked* and bobbed its head. "Yeah, yeah. She's getting into trouble." Maybe understanding the bird was easier than he'd expected. It really only ever had one thing to say. *Sabine's doing it again.* Tattling on the petite pickpocket was the whole of his discourse.

Noticing a woman scowling at him, Jean-Luc waved dismissively at the crow and moved further into the crowd. He'd given Sabine instructions. If she chose to find trouble instead of a tutor, what could he do about it? He should have known better. Giving her a direct order only assured she'd do the opposite. Jean-Luc was not responsible for her mistakes.

Even if the NOPD had set him aside for the time being, he knew his job. He protected the city, and something wasn't right here at the market. Warwick said they'd all seen the darkness, which was troublesome but also comforting. He'd been afraid the darkness appeared to him alone.

The woman with the scowl kept a wary eye on him as he merged into the crowd. Attempting to lose his NOPD stride, he tried to blend in, but it felt forced. He'd set himself apart as an observer for so long, then last fall, he was trapped in a black fog. It invaded him, and he'd felt watched ever since.

Delving into the shadows pervading the center of the market, snarls, growls, and yaps sounded around him. Vendors' eyes left their customers to watch him pass. None spoke. Their gazes broke as he passed, but the snarls followed.

The darkness returned, blurring his vision, leaving a veil over his view of the market. Suddenly, a black dog appeared, slavering behind a mask vendor. The animal brushed against the man's leg, and he stepped to the side, making room for the beast. It lunged, front paws hitting the table, shoving it forward. Customers moved back seemingly unconscious of the dog or their own movements.

On the opposite side of the aisle, a hiss came from a winged snake slithering across the banks of jewelry laid out in a booth. Something snagged Jean-Luc's pant leg, and he caught sight of black-tipped talons withdrawing under a table.

A sharp "*Caw, Caw,*" sounded overhead, and a glossy black wing brushed Jean-Luc's cheek. The veil over his vision evaporated, and customers shoved past, grumbling at him for blocking their path. Bertrand fluffed his feathers from atop a headless mannequin sporting a sequined sarong and bikini top.

"Bertrand," he spat the name like a curse. Some part of Jean-Luc knew he should thank the bird, but another part wanted to see what lurked on the other side. What hid in the shadows? How could he keep the city safe if he could only see half of it?

Bertrand *croaked* a curse of his own back at the detective. Or that's how Jean-Luc interpreted it.

"I can see why Sabine gets tired of you," he told it.

"*Creakee.*"

"Yeah, well, tell her I'm busy. She'll have to save herself for once," Jean-Luc responded as if he'd understood the bird. He had, or he thought he had. The dog and the serpent, the black talons and the crow talk all seemed like delusions, but he still heard the sound of clopping hooves.

Searching the crowd, Jean-Luc spotted a man with ram horns jutting out of his head. It wasn't a mask. The man stumbled to the edge of the pavilion, drunk or high. His skin was covered in a gritty black soot that left streaks on the silk scarves he passed. Jean-Luc followed. The strange young man had legs that crooked backwards. They were covered in fur and ended in hooves. Jean-Luc shoved past a woman and reached for the man, but another person passed in front of him. As he fought his way free, he saw the horned and hooved man step into the rain, and the illusion washed free. He was just a grubby man in worn corduroy pants.

Cursing himself for falling prey to another hallucination, Jean-Luc stomped back into the market crowd, shoving tourists aside.

At a booth in front of him, a young man in faded jean shorts and a stained t-shirt with a band he'd probably never heard on the front, ran his hand across a stack of leather wallets for sale. Keeping an eye on the vendor, who was helping another customer, the young man secreted a wallet into his back pocket.

This was no delusion, and a surge of righteous rage rose in Jean-Luc's gut. Later, he would wonder at the ferocity of the emotion caused by one petty thief when the city was fighting a much bigger war, but this thought didn't occur to him at the time.

He grabbed the young man's arm, wrenching it hard. His eyes wide with fear, the young man cried out and went limp. Jean-Luc dragged him to the edge of the market, where he could flag down an officer patrolling the area. The superintendent had ordered more officers as trouble rose. Petty thievery was not their main objective after a shooting and multiple stabbings had resulted in two deaths, just last week.

The man stumbled along beside him, whimpering. Jean-Luc gave him a shake to shut him up, and the man cried out. Tourists stopped to watch, and the man cowered in Jean-Luc's grip. Tendrils, which he hadn't noticed, scattered from his vision as he studied the terrified young man.

His shoulder, it didn't move right.

Oh Shit! Jean-Luc had dislocated it.

Tears streamed from the kid's eyes. He couldn't be over nineteen. "I'll tell the cops. I'll . . . I'll sue."

The tendrils darkened Jean-Luc's vision. He clenched his jaw, then drew close to the young man and spoke low. "You call out for the cops. And I'll have to tell them about all the loot in your pockets. Do you want that?"

The young man sniveled and flinched in pain.

Jean-Luc gripped the boy's shoulder with his left hand and shoved up, hard and fast with his right, popping the shoulder back into place. The boy screamed, and Jean-Luc let go.

The kid stumbled away, looking over his shoulder until he reached the street, then he ran, dodging between cars.

Ice ran through Jean-Luc's limbs.

What was he doing? He was a protector, not a predator. Or was he?

Chapter 9

CARMICHAEL

Carmichael unlatched the wooden gate with a screwdriver she kept in the glove box of her car. After weeks of trying to sneak up on the little thief, without success, Carmichael decided to try catching her at home. It hadn't been hard to discover where Sabine lived. Thibodeaux told her about the wretched woman's aunt dying in a false drug raid, back when he confided in her.

Somewhere along the way, she'd lost his trust. It was inevitable. His terminal integrity would get him killed one day, and she didn't plan on going down with him. She had a more fitting partner now. But she'd need to do away with Sabine to keep him on her side.

Carmichael shuddered at the thought of him turning on her.

Involuntarily, old memories of heartless corpses and blood splattered across walls barraged her mind. She stuffed it down, only for it to be replaced by the image of the short man in the red hat ripping a body apart.

Baylur, he'd finally given her his name. That denoted trust. Or she hoped it did. He would make a formidable ally. An ally with a monstrous appetite.

A devilish smile crossed her face as she imagined going toe-to-toe with him. The smile was immediately washed away when the storm clouds dumped their load on her with no prelude.

Cursing, she picked her way across the back of the house, sticking close to the clapboard siding. The eaves sent a curtain of water down, soaking her left arm before she reached the back stoop. An aluminum awning protected it from the worst of the rain. She crab-walked up the steps and peeked into the kitchen to be sure no one was home. She'd staked out the house for hours since losing track of Sabine at the market.

One minute she was there; the next she wasn't. Carmichael didn't know how she did it, but she had her suspicions. If she couldn't track the foxy thief, she'd lay in wait for her in her den. She chuckled at her metaphor as she popped the lock with her screwdriver.

She wrung as much of the water from her sleeve as she could, then eased the door open. A black streak shot past her head and into the house. Carmichael fell into a crouch, chin ducked to protect her face. When she opened her eyes, nothing moved in the space. She stepped across the threshold, all senses on high alert.

The kitchen's unusual, brilliant colors did nothing to diminish an overwhelming surge of malice. The walls creaked, and the floorboards moaned under her footsteps. A glint from the shadows above the cabinets gave her the impression the cottage watched her every move.

Her hand slipped under her damp suit coat to rest on her holster. Sweat ran down her brow, but she wrote it off as remnants of the rain caught in her hair. Circling the table, she crept down the hall, peering into each room as she passed. The house was empty.

A clatter came from the kitchen, and Carmichael ran on tiptoe to find the room remained empty. The clatter sounded again from above the cabinets. Probably rats, she thought with a shudder.

Ignore it, she told herself. On the far side of the table, she crouched. Hidden behind the plastic tablecloth, she waited for the fox to return to her den, smug in the belief that the clever thief couldn't evade her for long.

The green and gold medallion pattern on the linoleum tile had worn away except under the table. There, the seams between tiles were black, and the green and gold were stained brown, where the former owner had been found, murdered, last fall. Carmichael slid down to sit against the cabinet. She studied the stain as she waited, to keep her attention off the clicking of toenails above. Her shoulder itched where it met the cabinet, as if she could feel a rat about to climb down her arm.

The stain seemed to deepen. The hint of brown darkened until the outline was distinct. Something viscous seeped through the seams and spread to fill the shape with the crimson of fresh blood. As Carmichael stared in horror, it overflowed the bounds of the stain and ran toward her.

The front door slammed shut.

Startled, Carmichael looked back under the table to find the worn linoleum clean, free of any hint of stain. No blood.

A *squawk* from above brought her to her feet, gun aimed toward the opening. She didn't remember pulling it free of its holster. And wasn't sure in that moment if she intended on shooting the thief as she came into the kitchen. Is that where the blood had come from? A premonition.

Sweat dripped from her bangs and into her eyes. She couldn't write it off as rain this time.

"Sabine, is that you?" a person called from the front of the house.

Carmichael held her breath. She recognized that voice. It was that Armand woman who got away with murdering her last roommate, and now palled around with the thief. Did she live here, too?

"Don't fox out on me," Armand called down the hall. "We need to talk. I'm thinking about opening up the Sassy Witch. It's not like it will help Georgette escape jail. And I need a job. Are you listening to me?"

Footsteps came down the hall, and Carmichael slowly circled the kitchen until she stood out of sight beside the opening to the hallway. She steadied her revolver and eased off the safety. If she were prepared to take out Sabine, why not rid New Orleans of a murderer while she was at it?

She took a steadying breath and screamed as a black projectile struck her face. Talons raked at her jacket. Shrieks pierced her ears as a black beak jabbed for her eyes. She struck the bird with her gun, and it fell against the table. A crow. She'd dazed it, but its beady black eyes swiveled back to her.

Not waiting for a second attack, Carmichael dove for the back door. She jumped down the stairs, turned the corner, and hid behind a hydrangea. Rain battered its leaves, splattering her face. The back screen door slammed, and Megan Armand hollered across the backyard.

"You little chickenshit. You could at least stay and speak to me." With a grunt of disgust, Megan went back inside.

Carmichael wiped the water from her face, holstered her gun, and prepared to wait outside for the thief to come home. But the raucous crow would have none of that.

It swooped down and chased her away.

Chapter 10

SABINE

Hours passed, and the strip of golden light under the closet door dimmed. The latch clicked, and Sabine sprang from fox form to pissed off witch instantly. Ready to fight her way out. The door swung open to a Creole woman on the other side, the one who'd snatched her off the street.

With a hand on her hip, she cocked her head. "You look a mess. You been cutting up in there?"

Sabine was braced to run or fight or scream, but the woman's motherly demeanor didn't seem to call for any of it. Hadn't she heard any of Sabine's protests, her knocking, and screaming?

"Come on out." The woman waved her into the kitchen. "We gotta figure out how to deal with you." Six women sat around a wooden table in the cozy kitchen. All dark-skinned and stern-faced, eyes locked on Sabine.

The ruff of her neck rose in response, despite her human form.

"What's this?" she said with as much derision as possible. "A coven of witches?"

A woman at the end of the table with a lovely mane of salt-and-pepper dreadlocks cackled and slapped the tabletop in amusement. The woman beside her, with sable blown-out hair and a dimple in one cheek, gave her companion a sour look.

"Sissy, take this seriously."

"How can I, with that look on the child's face? Looks like one of them mad little Chihuahuas ready to gnaw somebody's ankle off." She broke into another round of laughter while Sabine stewed.

"I am not a child." Sabine crossed her arms, then realized how it looked and uncrossed them. "There's a ton of energy coming off of the lot of you. If you're not witches, then what are you?"

The women shared a look around the table, perhaps surprised she could feel it.

The woman who'd snatched her explained. "Perhaps you're feeling the energy of our ancestors. They've been with us quite a bit lately, trying to restore balance."

Another woman nodded confirmation.

"How exactly are you talking to these ancestors?" Sabine demanded. "And what balance are they concerned about?"

The woman with the dimple looked down her nose at Sabine. "We're priestesses of Voodoo. And if you haven't been able to notice the dark magic working its way through our city, then you clearly need more help than we thought."

"I was at the market, in the process of dealing with it, when I was snatched," Sabine said, her voice a lot more childish than she'd have liked. And to be honest, she hadn't really determined how to deal with the darkness, short of nipping at Thibodeaux's heels until she got him free of it.

"So it *is* centered on the market," her captor said.

A few nodded or made murmurs of agreement or groans of concern.

"What can you tell us of it?" A young woman with brilliant red lipstick and sharp eyes asked. She looked to be about Sabine's age, maybe a year or two older.

"Why don't you tell me why I'm being held captive?" Sabine countered.

One of them snorted, but she didn't catch which one.

"Sit down, child, and stop scowling," her captor said, pointing to a chair. "I'm Agnes. That's Sissy down there, Priestess Makayla next to her. Polly, Manbo Kate, and our youngest, Priestess Amara."

Polly was delicate-boned and tall and appeared to have transitioned recently. They had a Cupid's bow mouth, deep voice, and broad shoulders. They remained quiet, observing the others with inquisitive eyes.

Manbo Kate cocked her head and squinted, as if trying to make out who or what Sabine was. Or maybe she was just nearsighted. Her heavily creased face was framed by rows of earrings, and a collection of necklaces rested on her drooping bosom. She kept her eyes on Sabine.

"Agnes, you've got us all here. We've talked ourselves out while this rascal napped in the pantry. We made our decision. Best tell the girl what we intend."

Sabine stiffened, ready to run.

Agnes placed an iron grip on her shoulder before she could drop into fox form. "Sit a spell. Have a bite to eat. We'll chat, then you can leave."

Sissy gave her a wink and pushed a plate of cookies across the table to sweeten the deal. "Here, these'll take the edge off them angry nerves of yours while you tell us what had your ruff up when Agnes caught you."

The scent of cinnamon tickled Sabine's nose, and she salivated like Pavlov's pup. She plopped down, grabbed a cookie, and took a bite before begrudgingly answering.

"I was trying to protect my friend."

"From?" Sissy encouraged her.

"On the nights of the quarter moon, the French Market changes into a Faerie Market." Sabine paused. Did the Voodoo priestesses know about the fae? She continued in case they didn't. "It's located in the In Between, a sort of a halfway point between here and the Beyond. That's what blew up before the Mardi Gras parades. They called it a gas leak, but it wasn't."

Some murmured recognition. Others scoffed. They seemed split on the subject. She'd let them work that one out between themselves. It wasn't her job to prove anything to them.

Finishing the cookie in one bite, she continued. "This other market is rotten at the core, and it burst through to our side. It might do it again. Can you or your ancestors do anything to stop it? If not, you're just wasting my time."

"We'll consult them," Priestess Amara said. "But first, you have other concerns."

Priestess Makayla with the dimple leaned back in her chair. "You're a wild child in need of some guidance."

Anger warred with hunger in Sabine's gut, but maybe she could take advantage of the situation. She took another cookie and chose her next question carefully. "Could you talk to one of *my* ancestors?"

"Your aunt?" asked Agnes.

Sabine's breath caught. "You knew her?"

"*Of* her, but her spirit doesn't linger here."

Sabine's eyes burned, and she blinked the sensation away.

"We can give you something." Manbo Kate pulled a small pouch from her blouse and offered it to Sabine. It was fragrant with thyme and yard onions. "This'll offer some protection from the evil, unless it already has a hold on you."

Sabine reached for it. The woman gripped Sabine's hand and held it for several seconds, so that Sabine thought she'd have to wrestle it back. When the woman let go, she left the pouch behind. It had a leather cord to hold it around her neck.

"Gris-gris won't help as long as she keeps calling the dark to her," Priestess Makayla crossed her arms and rubbed her own gris-gris pouch between her thumb and forefinger.

"It can't hurt." Agnes sighed. "Now let's get to the business of what we're going to do with her."

"Nothing," Sabine said, popping out of her chair and heading for the door. "There's no way the seven of you get to decide what happens to me."

"Tsk. Tsk."

Sabine didn't turn to see who'd made the sound.

"Say you're not a child? Then don't act like one."

Sabine was pretty sure *that* was Agnes, but she was halfway down the corridor headed to the front of the house and didn't stop to find out if she was right.

No one followed. That made Sabine suspicious. Why didn't they try to stop her after keeping her trapped for a full day?

At the front of the house, Sabine stopped to take the measure of the place. The living room had two side tables, each with a lamp emitting warm light, a cozy couch, and a worn but well-polished coffee table. At the far end of the room, past the front door, stood a TV stand covered with a scarf. A candle with the image of the Virgin Mary burned, shedding light on three mismatched frames with black and white pictures. A green stoppered bottle sat to the side, and a few coins lay in the middle.

A home shrine, Sabine thought as she wrestled with the front door, which had swollen shut in its frame. She examined the pictures as she tugged. The portraits shared Agnes's features. Must be her ancestors.

Sabine had a pang of homesickness, but she shoved it down and heaved at the door while the priestesses continued discussing her in the kitchen.

"Should we offer her some goofer dust?" one asked.

"Lord, No! Child like that can barely control her own magic. Don't be giving her any more!" That one was definitely Priestess Makayla.

"I. AM. Not. A. Child," Sabine yelled with each tug at the door.

"I wouldn't be so sure about that," a crackly voice said as a ghostly hand reached through the door to grasp hers.

Sabine yelped, which sounded embarrassingly like a Chihuahua. She scrambled back, but the cool, dry hand holding hers came with her, as the rest of the body came through the door. The woman's translucent face gave Sabine a motherly smile. It was the same face framed on the altar. Sabine tried her best to shake off the spirit's grasp. As she fought it, another figure stepped through the face of the door, a short woman with long braids, the beads clacking softly. Sabine could see the door through the opalescent sheen of both women.

Reversing tactics, she barged forward, trying to ram her way through the two wraiths to reach the door. As ephemeral as they looked, they blocked her path like a brick wall, and, like a steam shovel, they pushed her back along the corridor as they advanced. More wraiths flooded in behind them. One came through the window and another down the chimney. A third sat on the shrine.

From the kitchen, the soft patter of sensible shoes on the hardwood floor advanced, and Agnes said, "You could've come straight to the kitchen, Momma. You don't have to come through the front door like a guest. We've discussed this."

The spirit still wore her motherly smile as she pulled Sabine gently along like an errant child. "Well, it never hurts to be polite."

Sabine scowled.

"I'm excited for your little family reunion, but I have things to do." Before she finished the sentence, darkness engulfed her, and she felt herself whisked away, while Sissy cackled up a storm.

Chapter 11

MEGAN

The sun had burned off the morning fog by the time Meg pulled up behind the Sassy Witch. The back door looked benign. No fangs. No hellfire. Layers of paint covered the heavy wooden door, thick enough that you could probably count the striations like the rings on a tree. Its ordinariness made it twice as suspicious.

She approached at an angle just to be safe. She'd debated bringing Sabine even though she'd been told not to, but Sabine would probably wreck something just for fun, to see if it ticked-off Georgette.

Sabine hadn't brought up the meeting in the last week. So maybe she didn't even remember Meg's phone call with Georgette. Although Meg had only seen her housemate in fox form for the last few days, which wasn't conducive to conversation. She'd disappear around mid-afternoon each day and not return until after the sun had come up the next morning, when she'd collapse in her room and sleep.

Meg would leave before Sabine woke to avoid talking to her and to make a quick pass by the market. This morning, she hadn't heard Sabine come in, but she left out the back and went around by the side gate to avoid passing by her room, just in case she was home.

What drew Meg to the French Market? She didn't really want to run into Baylur again, but she still had questions. She had the memories, but she needed to understand why. Why did she go with the fae in the first place? What was so broken in her that she would actively seek him out?

Meg didn't know what drew Sabine in, but the little witch resented the open-air market. She held it at least partly responsible for the abuse Meg had received in the Beyond, but Sabine kept going back, too, just like Warwick and Thibodeaux. Just like Meg. Warwick said the dark heart pulled on each of them. Maybe he was right. Meg wasn't about to ask Sabine, or the little witch would turn it back on her.

She didn't want another inquisition like, "Do you *want* to get abducted by the fae folk?" or, "Do you just crave the darkness like Thibodeaux?"

Meg didn't think so.

Putting the question aside for the moment, she squared off with the shop door. Meg didn't want Sabine around while she tried the Sassy Witch out for the first time since Georgette went to prison. It had taken her a week since the phone call to build up the courage. She didn't need Sabine barging in and setting something off. And she didn't think she could keep Sabine out if she really wanted in. Plus, she hadn't told any of them what else Georgette had asked her to do—find her enamel box and wait for instructions to bring it to the witch in jail. Hopefully, the wards would keep Sabine from following her in once she found out what Meg was up to. But first, Meg had to get inside.

Covering her hand with her sweater, she touched the knob. No sparks. No electric shock. No siren. She jiggled it. Nothing.

Counting to three, she turned the knob and jumped back. It slowly creaked open, like the forbidden door in a horror movie. Except it wasn't a haunted house. At least, she didn't think it was a haunted house. You never really knew in New Orleans. Luckily, it was daylight, a weak daylight, but still the sun was out. Fog drifted ominously from under the tree overhanging the door and flowed into the shop.

Meg shuddered. "That's it. I'm not going in."

"*Cr-r-rackk.*" Bertrand landed on a branch above the door.

"Did Sabine send you?"

"*Caw-Caw.*"

"I bet she didn't." Meg couldn't understand crow talk. Not like Sabine, but if you were around the two of them long enough, you could pick up the intricacies of her grunts and curses and his squawks and mutters. Sometimes, she pretended to understand just to annoy Sabine. Or because she felt left out of the conversation between the crow, Sabine, and Warwick.

Bertrand *muttered* at her as if daring her to go inside, or warning her away, or tattling on Sabine. Meg wasn't sure which, but it was definitely one of those.

"Don't tell Sabine, but I'm glad you're here." Meg stepped boldly up to the door, now that her feathered friend was there to witness any ghouls that might come after her. Tipping her head back, she asked, "I don't suppose you want to go first, do you?"

Bertrand started up a string of dialogue. "*Tock, tock, tock, mutter, mutter, mutter.*"

"I know. If I were Sabine, I'd just dive in. But she's brave."

"*Cr-r-rack, cr-r-rack.*"

"And reckless," she agreed as if actually conversing with the crow.

"*Creek.*"

"I opened the door. Maybe tomorrow I'll come back and open shop."

Bertrand launched off the door frame and strafed her cheek, his wingtips brushing her nose as he dove into the dark storage room at the back of the Sassy Witch shop.

"Fine." Stepping inside, Meg shut the door carefully. "Sometimes, I think you're as reckless as Sabine."

A quick tour of the shop showed everything was as she'd left it. Although the whole place had a musty odor, as if the heat hadn't been on to cycle the air since the witch was taken into custody. Meg checked the thermostat and flipped it on. The heat roared to life, and the fan whirred, spreading the smell of burnt dust, which successfully covered the musty odor.

Step one of breaking and entering done, Meg headed upstairs to see what Georgette's apartment looked like. Sabine had been up there, but Meg had never been invited. A Witch-Only Club. But no witches were available today. Berty *bugled* for her to hurry up. Or she decided that's what he meant.

"I'm coming." Taking the stairs two at a time, she reached the gaudy living area perfectly outfitted to the tastes of any wannabe-witch of New Orleans. A crushed velvet settee stood against the wall under a painting of a possibly French countryside. A lamp with a silk lampshade sat on a scalloped marble side table. Heavy velvet curtains were tied back with gold cords ending in huge tassels.

Bertrand perched on a tufted footstool in the middle of the room.

"Mlle. Georgette certainly commits to the whole cosplay thing, doesn't she?"

"*Rattle, rattle.*"

In the *boudoir*, scarves hung from chairs, lamps, bedposts, and a couple from the ceiling fan. Bertrand followed and landed on what Meg hoped was a fake fox fur stole hanging from a dressmaker's mannequin. Tiny paws hung down with black lacquered claws. The tail had a white tip. The glass eyes glistened as if they were wet and watching.

Bertrand pried at one with his beak.

"Ew! Leave it alone, please."

He moved on to picking at its fur.

Averting her eyes, Meg knelt on the tapestry rug to look under the bed. "She said to find an enamel box. There's two. Which one?"

She got no answer, so she grabbed both and hauled them out and hefted them onto the bed. They were shoebox-sized but remarkably heavy.

"*Cr-r-r-eek.*"

"I know, but she said, 'Don't open them.'"

Bertrand *muttered* to himself.

"You're right, I should open them."

He twisted his head, aiming one beady eye at her, which looked disturbingly similar to the fake fox's.

"What do you think she keeps in there that would help her get out of jail? A disappearing spell? A turn-into-mist spell? A screwing-with-your-mind spell? A bomb spell?" Meg turned her shoulder toward the bed to shield her chest, squinted, and snapped a box open. "Jewelry. It's just jewelry. What is she going to do with that?"

Bertrand didn't answer.

"Do you think they're for spellcasting?" Meg held up a gaudy amethyst ring to the light. "Maybe there's a spell in there. Do you think there's a spell in there?" She showed it to Bertrand, who *chattered* in response. Next, she pulled out a long strand of pearls and draped them around her neck. "What do you think? Be honest. Too much for day wear?"

Bertrand turned his head away, looking out the window.

"You're right. Too much."

A sharp rap came at the shop door downstairs.

Meg shrieked, dropped the pearls, which came unstrung and scattered across the floor.

A second knock assured her it hadn't been her imagination.

Bertrand *creaked* as if distressed. Meg snatched up a handful of pearls, threw them into the box, shoved both boxes under the bed, and shut the bedroom door.

The knocking increased.

Bertrand landed on Meg's shoulder. She gently lifted him off and set him on the back of the settee. "You stay up here until I find out what's going on down there."

Meg leapt down the stairs and swung around the door frame to the dark shop. She had a view straight down the aisle, between T-shirt kiosks, shelves of tarot cards, and racks of crystals to the front door. An older Creole man pounded on the glass. Bertrand landed back on her shoulder.

The man's eyes locked with hers, and he motioned for her to unlock the door, and quick. He looked intense, but not deranged.

"Thanks. He's seen us now," she whispered to the crow, then raised her voice so the man could hear it. "We're closed. We won't be open for another hour."

Without taking his eyes from Meg's, he shifted so that she could see he had the arm of another man wrapped around his shoulder. The second man slumped against him, probably drunk. She was definitely not opening the door. The drunken man's head lolled to the side, revealing a horn that twined from his left temple and around a tufted ear.

Bertrand *shrieked*.

"Oh, Crap!"

Chapter 12

WARWICK

With the tall one away and the witchling in hiding, Warwick could move about the city without fear of one or the other quizzing him. He had warned them away from the darkness, yet they persisted in bungling towards it. He had done what he could for these feeble-minded creatures. Now, he must take care of his own matters.

Black talons reached from cracks in the building's facade to snag upon Warwick's coat. He hissed curses in the high language of the goblin court, and the vermin retracted their gnarled fingers. If the Night Court did not rid itself of these vermin, they would soon break through into the human world. Warwick walked close to the centuries-old brick walls to evade the pedestrians and to hide amidst the shadows cast by the balconies overhead, but also because their age comforted his homesick soul.

If any of the sightless humans noticed him, they quickly looked away, which suited his purposes well. He followed directions to the Midnight Jazz Club mapped out for him by the Lady Megan. He had studiously taken notes as she retold stories of the night she first met the troublesome fae, Baylur. Even with the map in hand, Warwick's sense of direction was knocked askew on this side of the In Between, where the sun rose in the wrong direction and the river ran backwards. But he was a goblin. He found his way even in this misguided land.

A glamor concealed the building, but it did not fool him. Warwick saw through the illusion of the cracked plaster, broken shutters, and chained doors to the vibrant club beneath.

Bertrand circled overhead, a silhouette against the bright sunlit sky. Warwick ignored his cry and stepped from the human street and onto a sidewalk lit by starlight. The In Between held this place at perpetual midnight.

The Midnight Jazz Club, a piece of the In Between favored by the fae, did not normally welcome goblins. However, the youngest of the goblin princes had made acquaintances with the club's owner. The prince was not only allowed entrance, but welcomed. Warwick did not understand their arrangement, but he hoped to make use of it. While Megan, Thibodeaux, and Sabine dispersed to carry out their futile agendas, Warwick had other, more important considerations.

Lanky, languid, fae draped themselves against the door frames, either choosing to ignore him or affecting sneers at his approach. It mattered not to Warwick. It would only become a problem if one of them attempted to stop him. As he boldly walked through the double doors, a fae broke from the group of dancers and dared to confront him.

Warwick stopped, squared his own shoulders, and flexed his fingers. These seemingly frail creatures were stronger than they appeared, but no match for a goblin. Warwick lifted his chin and sighted down his nose at the creature. Its eyes sparked like amethysts. Scales glittered along the fae's throat and across its shoulders. Its narrow chest heaved like bellows as the fae attempted to assert its authority.

The enchanting piano music ceased. The saxophone followed with a trailing note that hung in the air above them. The dancers came to a halt and turned en masse to face them.

Warwick took a quick survey of the room, noting that the goblin prince was not present this evening. Well, Warwick would make do. He resumed his path towards the bar. The fae showed no sign of relenting. If need be, Warwick would merely walk through the creature. Nothing could stop a goblin, save stone itself.

Before goblin and fae met, an authoritative voice cut through the silence.

"This goblin is under house protection until further notice." The woman who spoke had a regal bearing. She held reign behind a copper bar. Her skin a warm brown. Her eyes dark and sharp. Her hair formed a magnificent halo of curls around her lovely face. Warwick could see how she might have mesmerized the goblin prince. Her clientèle parted, allowing him a narrow passage.

When Warwick reached the bar, he bowed deeply, showing appropriate deference to an amour of the goblin Court.

"If I may introduce myself, I am Warwick, once of the High Goblin Court."

"*Once?* That sounds like it has an interesting story attached," she said with the slightest of smiles on those lush lips.

"Forgive me, ma'am. That tale must wait for another time. I am here on business."

The smile spread across her face, and her eyes lit up. "Very well. I am Zulu de Bonaire, owner of the Midnight Jazz Club, but I think you already know that. What is it I can do for you before this innocent looking bunch of fae turns on the both of us?"

Warwick would never have classified a room full of fae as innocent, but now was not the time to debate perceptions. He did not doubt that they would turn on him and the owner, if only to amuse themselves. "I had hoped to speak to Prince Pierre III. Would you be expecting him in this evening?"

"It's always *night* at the Midnight Jazz Club. And no one can reliably predict the moment a prince might decide to appear. Although I appreciate the fact that you think I am worthy of keeping the royal schedule."

Warwick inclined his head in acknowledgement. He would not be indelicate. He knew better than to repeat rumors of the prince spending an inordinate amount of time in this fae establishment and in the house of Zula de Bonaire.

"If I may," she asked, "why look for him here? Why not seek him in the Beyond?"

Warwick certainly would not explain his reasons for avoiding the Beyond.

The hum of conversation hushed behind him. He turned in time to see a tall goblin with flaming green eyes and broad shoulders wave a greeting to the musicians. A trumpet blare sounded in response. Then the prince caught sight of Warwick at the bar with Zula. The question in his eyes was first asked to her, then to the goblin, confirming the rumors that the young prince held her in the highest regard.

"Well. Well. Well," Zula said with a broad smile. "It looks like your lucky night, Master Warwick."

"Indeed," he said, and yours as well, by the look on your face, Warwick thought. Turning to the prince, Warwick gave a deep bow equal to the station he once held in the goblin court, showing respect to one of the royal family. It would not earn him his place back, but it did not hurt to show respect.

"Master Warwick, what brings you here? Are you seeking work in a fae nightclub?"

Warwick blanched at the suggestion, barely catching himself before letting it show on his face. He had not succeeded, judging by Zula de Bonaire's expression. Her sardonic expression reminded him of the witchling. Perhaps it was just a human affectation, and Megan Armand was simply unique in her ability to control her features. The thought raised the tall one in his estimation.

"Although it would be a great honor to work for Lady de Bonaire, I have come for Your Highness's counsel."

Zula's scowl relaxed, but her eyes remained wary. "Can I get the two of you a drink while you talk?"

The prince raised his eyebrows to Warwick, who gave the slightest shake of his head. Prince Pierre smiled fondly at his amore before replying. "No, thank you, Zula. It looks like Warwick and I will need to discuss this outside."

Zula's scowl returned full force. Warwick had not only insulted her bar, he had also robbed her of the unexpected pleasure of seeing her amour. For this, he was sorry. She had the affection of a goblin prince. Therefore, crossing her could come with unpleasant consequences.

The prince gestured for Warwick to lead the way outside. Which was probably best. Having the prince at his back was comforting in this fae den.

Once outside, the prince leaned against the wall, ready to listen.

"If Your Highness will forgive me, I feel it is best not to discuss such a sensitive issue so close to others."

"You mean the fae? Would you rather step into the human world?"

"No, Your Highness. Is not there somewhere else we might speak?" Warwick knew he was not allowed in the goblin realm, but he also knew the prince had access to other spaces.

Prince Pierre studied him, his brow furrowed. "Does this affect the goblin court?"

Warwick looked around for prying eyes and attentive ears. Seeing no one, but still wary, he nodded. "Perhaps, Your Highness."

"Well then, the Elsewhere it is." The prince raised his hand and snatched away the neon light, leaving the two of them in a darkness. "Explain," he said, his tone sharp.

"I wish to know what recompense I might pay that would allow me back into the king's good graces."

"You want to come home," the prince's voice mellowed. "To be banned from King Phillip's court was a harsh sentence. Perhaps too harsh, but he made the decree, and he does not oft go back on such an edict as exile."

"I understand, Your Highness." Warwick inclined his head respectfully. "Would it please His Majesty to have this sordid business at the market addressed?"

The prince's sharp tone returned. "Weren't you banned from the market as well?"

"I might still be able to assist." Surely, he could find a way in past the minotaur.

"Settling the market would certainly be a boon."

Warwick hesitated before adding, "It could prove dangerous for certain humans."

"And this disturbs you?" Prince Pierre seemed puzzled at Warwick's concern.

"I feared since you were fond of the . . ."

"Of Zula, a human," the prince finished Warwick's thought, his voice as cold and sharp as a shard of ice. "Zula is under my care. Any action that puts her in peril forfeits your life."

Warwick took a step back and bowed deeply in subservience. "Of course, Your Highness."

The prince's face grew grim. But business was business. The prince answered to the king, human amour, or not.

"I will see to it," Warwick assured him.

"Yet I cannot say if even the cleansing of the market would be enough." Prince Pierre inclined his head, acknowledging the sorrow in losing access to the goblin court. "But it is a start."

"It is a start," Warwick echoed as his gut clenched. He would have to find a grander act of contrition to salve the king's ire.

Chapter 13

SABINE

Once the Voodoo priestess's ancestors released Sabine, she wavered on her feet, attempting to regain her balance. The sun rose swollen and heavy, dragging itself out of the murky waters of the bayou. Tall, shaggy cypress trees rose to either side. Their knobby knees thrust up through the mulch. Her slippers sank into the damp earth. Water seeped in, and her toes squelched.

How she had gotten from Priestess Agnes's home to the edge of the bayou, she had no idea. The crowd of spectral ancestors that had engulfed her and transported her to the bayou was nowhere in sight.

Somewhere in the canopy overhead, a gray heron croaked in disapproval and took flight. Its shadow raced across the placid waters. A ripple started a few feet out from the land and made its way towards the shore. A set of eye ridges rose above the water's edge, followed by nostrils. The gator's head had to be eighteen inches long.

"You are one big boy." Sabine inched backwards.

"Don't mind him. He doesn't bite unless he's hungry." A young woman with rich brown skin and soft brown eyes smiled at her.

Sabine was sure she hadn't been there a moment before, but she refused to show her surprise. "How do you know if he's hungry?"

"Well, if he goes to gnawing at your leg, that's a pretty good sign." The woman's smile was disarming, which immediately put Sabine's guard up. "Come on up to the house. Sit a spell and have some sweet tea."

Unless Sabine planned on wading out into the water with the alligator, going inland with the woman seemed to be her only option. She had a slow, easy gait. Her hips swayed in the lazy manner of someone who had nowhere to go and the whole day to get there.

The bayou appeared to wrap around both sides of the spit of land where they walked. Sabine scanned the area for potential dangers as well as potential escape routes. "Are we on an island or peninsula?"

"Depends on the time of day and the day of the week." The woman's speech was as languid as her walk.

"So today, what would it be?" Sabine tried her best to keep the irritation out of her voice. This woman sounded as cryptic as Warwick. Maybe she was fae, although she didn't have the look of one. Not that Sabine had seen many outside of the In Between.

"Oh, I'd say it's feeling itself to be an island. But that could change."

Can't anyone give a straight answer to anything anymore?

In front of them, an old clapboard house with weathered siding nestled under the overhanging Cyprus limbs. Three steps led up to a porch, its railing draped with honeysuckle. The sweet smell filled the air as they climbed onto the porch. Two rockers sat between the door and a window thrown open despite the time of year.

It was then Sabine realized that the chill which had draped itself over New Orleans for the past month was replaced by a balmy breeze here. Crickets sang as if it were mid-spring and not the edge of winter. Which would explain the bright yellow flowers lacing the honeysuckle vines.

"Have a seat. I'll get us some tea," her guide gestured to a chair.

Instead, Sabine walked to the far end of the porch and peeked around the corner for signs of a road or a car or a boat. Nothing. She turned to go to the other side and was surprised to find an elderly woman sitting in one of the rockers. She held the cuff of a blouse between her fingers, the rest of the shirt draped across her lap. She fastidiously threaded a button onto a needle and attached it to the cuff. Not paying any mind to Sabine.

The worn boards of the porch squealed in protest with Sabine's every step. Yet Sabine hadn't heard the woman come out and have a seat. However, now that she saw her, she could hear the slow creak of the rocker. Had she been there in the shadows and Sabine missed her?

On a little table between the two rockers was a lacquered wooden tray with two glasses of iced tea. Condensation dripped down the sides, forming a puddle beneath them, as if they'd been waiting for Sabine for a while.

Without lifting her eyes from her mending, the older woman said, "Go on, have a seat so we can chat for a bit." Without waiting for Sabine to follow instructions, she continued chatting, almost as if to herself. "I hear you been quite a handful. Got the Voodoo ladies all in an uproar. You want to tell me about it?"

Still standing, Sabine started ranting. "I haven't had any dealings with the priestesses. They snatched me off the street while I was in the middle of trying to—"

The woman patted the air, indicating for Sabine to sit. And she was setting, before she realized she had.

"What am I doing here?"

"Seems you needed someone to talk to. This is a good place to do it. Nice and quiet but for the buzzing of the bugs." The woman put down her sewing and picked up her tea. She took a sip, her movements just as languid as those of the younger woman. Sabine wondered if they were related. "Tell you what, you tell me some of your stories and I'll share some of mine. What do you think about that?" The woman leaned back in her rocker.

It didn't seem like such a bad idea. Although Sabine was pretty sure she was in a hurry to get something done. She just couldn't quite remember what at the moment. She took up the iced tea and had a sip. The cold liquid went down her throat, quenching a thirst she hadn't realized she had.

They rocked for a minute, and Sabine watched the sun rise between the trees. Its rays shone through the branches, lighting the pollen as if it were on fire.

"The priestesses, they seem to think I need training in magic. But I'm a witch. I should know magic, right?"

"Even a baby bird could use someone to help nudge it out of the nest."

What was that supposed to mean?

As Sabine wondered whether this conversation was going anywhere or not, and if she just needed to make a run for it, the woman suddenly sat bolt upright and snipped her scissors right above Sabine's knee.

"What the hell?"

"None of that here, child." The woman sat back in the chair and picked up her tea again. How had she moved that fast? Sabine checked the edge of her jumper to see if the woman had cut a notch in it. It was intact, and she leaned back cautiously.

A twig reached out from the vines along the railing. It wriggled, seeking the sunlight maybe. When it came within a hand's span of her, Sabine could see it wasn't part of the vine but a shadow. It reached for the fingers she had draped over the arm of the rocker. Just before it touched, the woman snipped it again, and it snapped back into the vines.

The woman tutted. "They were right about the darkness. It sure does seem to have a fondness for you." She sat back in her rocker and worked on the collar of a different shirt, relaxed as if she'd never moved.

"What makes the shadows do that? And how did you stop it? Are you a witch? Are those scissors magic?" Sabine leaned forward, watching the vine for any more errant twigs of shadow.

"That's a lot of questions, and we haven't even started telling stories yet. Why don't you tell me how it is you got to be in New Orleans on your own? A young witch with no training." The woman rocked and stitched, her eyes on her work. The creases in her face deepened with the rising sun.

Sabine couldn't believe she'd been kidnapped and dragged to this island to tell stories. She opened her mouth to tell the woman as much, but what came out was something else.

As the crickets sang and the ice settled in the glasses, Sabine found herself telling the woman how her mother had begun to waste away. How she and her father hadn't known what to do to help her. How her mother had told Sabine that it was her time. There was nothing to worry about. But she left her daughter without ever teaching her a bit of witchcraft. Not a single spell. Not even a way to take care of herself against the magic that was creeping into New Orleans from the other side.

She left Sabine and her father alone with no instructions. Her father, wrapped in confusion, not knowing what to do with his feral child, had sent her to the city to find her mother's sister. Sabine had been there only a day when someone killed her aunt for the crime of helping the helpless.

A sob broke from Sabine's chest. Wrenched out of her throat, it erupted into the air before Sabine could catch it. She scrubbed at her cheeks, inflamed with anger at being left, at sorrow unspent, and with embarrassment at letting it all loose in front of this stranger.

She spoke with hiccupping breaths. "How did you do that? How did you make me say all that? I'm not even sad, really. I don't know why I'm crying."

A warm hand patted her shoulder and handed her a fresh glass of tea. It was the younger woman smiling down at her. She sat down in the rocker where the older woman had been just a moment before.

"Crying won't quench that fire in you. Tears are holy. They cleanse the shadows inside that stop you from burning bright. Don't you worry."

"I'm not worried." Sabine hiccupped. "Where did the other woman go?" She must've been her mother or grandmother. They looked too much alike not to be related.

"Just you and me here. The stories we share stay just between the two of us. Although I'd recommend you find someone you trust to share them with back home every now and then. It's good for you."

Sabine waited for her hiccups to subside before speaking again. "I thought I was here to learn how to control magic."

"Honey, magic's not for you to control."

Sabine was about to protest when a snap of scissors clicked right behind her ear. She jerked to see who was behind her, but no one was there.

Chapter 14

MEGAN

Meg wasn't sure if she was doing the right thing by opening the door to the Sassy Witch shop and letting the injured satyr inside, but she couldn't leave him out there. The older Creole man helped him inside, introducing himself simply as Ol' Ben.

"Trouble at the market," he said, transferring the satyr's arm to Meg's shoulder.

"Is he hurt?" she asked. "What do I do with him?"

"Miss Beauchamp'll be along when she's able. You just sit tight." Ol' Ben tipped his hat to her and left.

Without further instruction, Meg stumbled through the shop with the semiconscious satyr, knocking displays over as they went.

On the stairs, one hoof dragged behind as he leaned against her, and they struggled to the top. Both were drenched in sweat and breathing in gasped breaths by the time they reached the second floor. Meg led him to Georgette's bed, where he collapsed across the velvet coverlet. His horns scratched the antique wood headboard as Meg tried to arrange him, horns and hooves, onto the bed.

"Georgette won't be pleased by that. Maybe we should've tried the settee." Meg said half to herself, half to the bird.

The satyr had passed out. So, he wasn't going to answer. She could imagine Sabine gloating over the damaged furniture. She probably would have arranged for it to happen, Meg thought, then felt guilty for thinking ill of her friend.

Bertrand strutted up and down the satyr's calf from his hoof past the ankle joint to the knee and back as if he needed to convince himself that this creature was real. Meg shooed him off, and he fluttered to the top of the window shade, where he *clicked* nervously.

"Could you stop that? You sound like a bomb about to go off."

Bertrand twisted his head to the side and gave her the eye.

Unwilling to just sit and wait for this mysterious Beauchamp to appear, Meg called Thibodeaux. He answered on the first ring.

"Megan?"

"I'm at the Sassy Witch and need help."

"Be right there," was all he said before the line went dead.

Well, that would have to do. Neither Warwick nor Sabine had a cellphone, and she needed help figuring out what to do with the creature. His muscled chest, covered in a fine velvety fur, rose and fell at irregular intervals. Meg worried that he might stop breathing altogether before Thibodeaux got there.

"Should I go open the shop, or wait on the detective?" Meg fluttered a hand over the satyr's arms and neck, checking all the visible skin for wounds, but couldn't find any. Although his skin felt hot to the touch. "Do creatures tend to run hot?"

That made her think of the cold fae, Baylur, and her face flushed. Well, maybe satyrs were different. Surely they were.

"He doesn't look injured. But something's wrong." The creature's face and fur were covered in a thin layer of gritty soot with pale streaks cut through it. "Trouble at the market, that's not much info, is it?" Meg wondered if it was something new. If the market were about to burst wide open.

Bertrand refused to answer.

Downstairs, Meg opened the back door and left it ajar, hoping that would prevent any wards from activating and zapping Thibodeaux or the Beauchamp lady. Then she went back up to the bedroom with a damp washcloth and wiped the black soot from the satyr's brow, leaving it a pale shade of faun. She ran her fingers lightly through the hair on his brow. The grit tumbled free, leaving his silky locks a pale reddish brown.

"It's almost like he was in a fire with all this soot."

Bertrand *squawked*, and heavy footsteps creaked on the stairs.

"Megan, are you up there?"

Thank God. It was the detective.

"Yes," she yelled back. "We're up here in Georgette's boudoir."

He pounded up the stairs.

"You got here awfully fast," Meg said when the detective appeared in the doorway.

"I was close by. What's going on?"

Meg stepped back to reveal the satyr.

Thibodeaux startled, and his face clouded. He shook his head and looked away from the creature. "Where's Sabine?"

Meg huffed in exasperation. "How should I know? Ask him?"

Bertrand fluffed his wings and *tocked*.

The detective looked at the crow skeptically. "I'm not sure he knows."

The crow *shrieked*, but they both ignored him.

"Yeah, just like the rest of us. No one ever knows where she is, which is why I called *you* to help with *this*." She gestured at the poor creature suffering on the bed, but Thibodeaux was looking about the room as if he might find a clever fox hiding under the bed or behind the curtains. She tried to direct his attention to the problem at hand. "What should we do?"

The detective opened and closed the door to the closet and then the bathroom. "How long has it been since you've seen her?"

"In fox or witchy-bitch form?"

"Either," he said, surveying the living area from the bedroom doorway.

"Awhile. Did you two go at each other again?" Meg crossed her arms and glared, which was lost on the oblivious man. The satyr jerked and moaned, and she went to its side to stroke its forehead until it settled back down.

Thibodeaux peeked past the curtains. "Has Georgette called again, asking for anything?"

"If she had, I'd ask if she was okay with a wounded creature on her comforter. You know. See if she minded. Or to ask," Meg's words got punchy. "What. To. Do. About. It?"

At last, Thibodeaux cut his eyes to the creature. The detective's brow creased, and his eyes darkened.

Bertrand *tocked* and bobbed his head.

Meg took an involuntary step back and tripped over an antique wooden chair covered in velvet. Before she could fully recover, her phone rang. She looked at Thibodeaux, then back at her phone.

"It's the jail," Meg whispered, as if someone might hear.

Thibodeaux's muscles tensed like he were holding something back by force. Meg was about to swipe to cancel the call when he barked, "Answer it."

And so, against her better judgment, she did.

"Uh, hello."

Thibodeaux took the phone. "What is it you want?"

"I want out," the heavily accented voice snapped back.

"That's not going to happen," he told the witch.

Meg put herself between the satyr and the detective, listening for Georgette's reaction.

"We shall see." The witch's French accent did nothing to soften the toxin in her voice.

Thibodeaux's scowl morphed into a devious smile. "I tell you what, you tell me what you know about what's going on at the market, and maybe we can see about a courtesy jailbreak for our favorite witch."

"*Caw. Caw*," Bertrand unfurled his wings for emphasis.

"N-O," Meg mouthed, but the detective's grin didn't relent. She performed the universal cut-it-off motion.

Georgette's voice lowered to a seductive tone that Meg couldn't make out, but Thibodeaux seemed pleased. Too pleased.

"She's right here. Hope to see you soon, Mademoiselle." Thibodeaux handed the phone back to Meg. "She wants to talk. I've got to make arrangements." He headed for the stairs.

Meg hit 'Mute' and followed. "Arrangements for what?"

"For a visit with our lovely friend." The detective had an ugly smile. Meg had never seen him like this, and she didn't like it.

"If you mean Georgette, I . . . I don't even want to know what you're up to."

"Good."

Meg caught the back door before he closed it. "What about the satyr?"

"It's not real. You're having a delusion."

"He's not a delusion," she said through gritted teeth.

Thibodeaux waved a dismissive hand in the air and left.

Bertrand soared past her and headed in the opposite direction.

"Fine, you both go chasing shadows. I'll just be here tending to a very real, very sick satyr."

After yelling that down the street, Meg nervously checked to see if anyone had heard, then closed the door and locked it. Remembering the phone in her hand, she tapped to unmute and immediately regretted it.

The witch's cackle sounded through the speaker like the startled scream of a murder of crows.

Chapter 15

THIBODEAUX

If that witch actually thought she could get Megan Armand to walk into the prison and spring her out, well... She might be right. Her demands could play right into his plan for a more permanent punishment for the Mlle. Georgette than jail. That should appease Sabine.

It worried him that Megan hadn't seen or talked to her. So, the petite thief wasn't just mad at him. She was mad at everyone, which made her impulsive. She was always impulsive, but anger made her more so than usual. Who knew what trouble she would get herself into? And he'd waved off Bertrand when he'd tried to warn him.

Right now, he had to set things into play for Megan to get in to see the incarcerated witch. Then he'd hunt for Sabine.

At the Sassy Witch shop, Jean-Luc had immediately recognized the odd creature with horns and hooves as the one from the market. He'd assured Megan she was imagining it, but he knew she knew better. Jean-Luc had the uneasy feeling that she felt safer alone with the strange creature than she did with him. A disturbing thought, but he reminded himself that her sense of self-preservation hadn't been particularly accurate in the past. Maybe she felt more comfortable around creatures since her travels into the Beyond.

Black tendrils clouded his vision, and Jean-Luc prayed the traffic stayed steady and the traffic light stayed green. He made it through the intersection, and his vision cleared. Cursing under his breath, he scanned the surrounding cars to see how close he'd come to a crash. He kept trying to convince himself that he had control of the darkness inside him, but he knew it for a lie.

Blocks passed without incident, and Jean-Luc parked on the street facing the austere building housing the headquarters of the New Orleans Police Department. It had seemed so majestic when he'd first joined the force. Though even then, it had been menacing enough for pedestrians to steer clear while officers filtered in and out, no longer noticing the exterior. Jean-Luc had been among them a short few months ago.

Today, it loomed over the corner, judging him. Its tall, narrow windows, separated by columns of concrete, gave it the feel of a fortress, one he wouldn't breach, not today. His mandatory leave didn't banish him from the building. Although the superintendent had made it clear, she did not intend to see him back before he was called in.

Jean-Luc circled to the southeast corner of the back lot, where he leaned against an old, but well cared for, Honda sedan to wait. He withdrew a pocket watch with a cracked face to check the time. It remained motionless. Putting it back in his pocket, he checked the time on his phone. Wouldn't be long now.

"Son of a gator," came the rusty voice of Officer Wilhelm. "Wondered how long it'd take before you showed up."

"If you answered my calls, I wouldn't have to." Jean-Luc shook the man's hand amicably. "Could've shown up at your house, but we both know Glenda would have me in for dinner and a third degree."

Wilhelm huffed. "No lawyer could beat that woman at cross-examination." Their eyes met briefly, then Wilhelm dug in his pocket for his keys as he talked. "She didn't buy that story about you going home for some R-n-R. No one does."

"From what I hear, it's all over the internet." Within a day of the incident, cellphone video had been posted of Jean-Luc tearing the Eros float apart in the middle of the Mardi Gras parade—the real reason he was on leave from the force.

Wilhelm opened his door but paused before getting inside. "Can't always believe what you hear. Or what you see either. Glenda don't, and to tell the truth, neither do I."

"It was close enough to the truth to warrant sending me home. Superintendent did the right thing."

Wilhelm shifted his weight as if he were about to get in, but didn't. "I suppose you're here, where Harris is sure to see and report back to your protégé, for a reason."

Jean-Luc laughed out loud, and Wilhelm joined him.

"Yeah, that kid hasn't been here a minute past his shift since I've known him." The tension broken. Wilhelm looked him in the eye. "What you need, Luc?"

"Want to meet elsewhere and get a coffee? Talk a minute?"

"No, best not. Make it quick. Tell me what you need, and I'll do what I can. You know I will. Just like I know you won't ask me for anything I'll regret."

Jean-Luc flinched at the comment but covered it with a cough. Wilhelm's eyes narrowed. The detective hurried to explain so his fellow officer wouldn't ask too many questions about the ethics of his request. "The woman, Georgette, says she's a witch. She called her employee today, demanding she come to the jail. Are visitations authorized?"

"She's considered a security risk. It would take prior approval, but it's possible. This employee—do you suspect them of colluding?"

"No, the witch wants to make sure the woman, Megan Armand, is watching her shop until she gets out. I'm hoping Ms. Armand can get some information out of her about her accomplice in the murders." That sounded legit and was at least half the truth.

Wilhelm nodded slowly. "I don't see any danger in a visitation then."

"Not unless she's a real witch?" Jean-Luc faked a laugh.

Wilhelm did not join him.

"I'll make sure it doesn't blow back on you," Jean-Luc said, and he meant it at the time.

"You think you can do that?"

"Tell you what. Just forget it." Jean-Luc felt the darkness rising and ducked his head.

"Settle down. I taught you to check all the angles, didn't I? Don't think I forgot how to do it myself."

Jean-Luc took a couple of deep breaths and blinked his eyes clear. "Yeah. I get it. I guess I'm hoping she can shed some light on whatever's happening at the French Market."

"You know this ain't your job at the moment, Luc, neither is the murder investigation. Carmichael's in charge."

"So, I'm just supposed to stop caring?"

"I don't suppose so."

"I'm checking all the angles, too, and it don't look good. Things are happening that the NOPD can't handle by conventional means."

Wilhelm's chest rose and fell as he thought it through. "Even the Voodoo priestesses are circulating warnings. It's not like them to offer advice unless it's asked for."

His friend patted his chest over a small bulge under his uniform. Jean-Luc wondered if he wore a gris-gris pouch. Wilhem wasn't superstitious, but his wife didn't make distinctions between the mysterious and the miraculous. And no New Orleans native was stupid enough to underestimate the practitioners. They weren't like the ones on television. To tell the truth, Jean-Luc didn't really know much about the true religion, but he sure didn't disrespect it.

"Look. I'm trying to clean things up, not make another mess. Nothing like the parade." Jean-Luc felt the muscle in his cheek twitch. He knew how shady it all sounded. He didn't do shady shit. Wilhelm knew that, but Jean-Luc wasn't sure that was still a fact. He made a quick calculation. "If you like, I'll keep you in the loop."

"Don't. I'll get the visit cleared. Tell this *employee* to ask for me and I'll give her visiting hours and protocol."

"Thanks." Jean-Luc nodded and turned to leave.

"Luc."

"Yeah?"

"Don't take this wrong. But I don't want to see you around here again until the superintendent clears you. Right?" Wilhelm didn't wait for an answer as he got in and shut the door.

"Right," Jean-Luc answered as he walked out of the lot with a heavy heart. Old friends are hard to make and harder to lose.

Chapter 16

MEGAN

Three days and three nights passed while Meg sat alone over the shop with the satyr. Thibodeaux never showed back up to help. Sabine didn't come looking for her. And Warwick was probably sulking in the shed behind Sabine's house. Even Bertrand didn't come back to check on her. Meg was on her own. She didn't dare leave the satyr alone.

Luckily, Georgette had a freezer full of expensive takeout from various Parish restaurants and plenty of cash for delivery when she ran out. Meg ate the witch's food, drank her wine, and sat at the bedside. She'd felt abandoned and helpless since the satyr stumbled through the door.

The first night, she'd spent watching his tawny chest rise and fall in a ragged rhythm. In the wee hours of the morning, the creature's eyes had fluttered. His brow had broken out in a sweat, and he mumbled an incoherent fever dream, seemingly full of horrors. The last few hours, he'd settled into a restless sleep and remained there despite Meg's efforts to rouse him.

The next night, she tried to nap on the settee, but it was way too short and she was way too long. She woke with a crick in her neck. Last night, she'd caved and carefully climbed onto the bed beside the creature. After watching his fitful breathing, she passed out, wondering if this Beacham or Beauchamp would ever show up.

After the sun decided to rise for another day, the obvious solution finally slammed into Meg's addled brain. Magic. It could help. But there was no Sabine nor Georgette available. Meg hadn't talked to her roommate since the morning Thibodeaux and Warwick met with them in Sabine's kitchen. And she hadn't seen Sabine since the day before the satyr came knocking at the shop door. But damn it, this was a magic shop.

Surely there was magic lying around somewhere that could help. Meg spent the morning searching Georgette's apartment for anything that might work. If any of the jewels held magic, Meg didn't know how to use them, and there was no instruction manual on hand.

That left the shop, Meg chanced leaving the creature alone to go downstairs to look. Hours passed while she dug through the racks and carousels. She was scrounging through unpacked boxes behind the counter when the doorbell sounded. Why Mlle. Georgette had designed a magical ward to sound exactly like an electric doorbell, Meg would never know.

She hadn't thought to check whether Thibodeaux had locked the door when he left. She hadn't thought of much of anything but keeping the satyr alive. She stood to tell the customer they weren't open, but the words stuck in her throat.

Chapter 17

CARMICHAEL

The shop on the corner had a predictably purple and black sign reading *SASSY WITCH*. From the goods displayed in the window—black T-shirts with spiky lettering, crystals strung on chains, and an advertisement for palm readings—this shop was no different from any of the others. Except this one employed the current housemate of a clever nuisance, Sabine Domingue.

After two days staking out Sabine's house, Carmichael hadn't seen either woman come or go. They were obviously holed up somewhere else, and she would bet that somewhere was the witch's shop.

An electric bell chimed as Carmichael entered. She was not there on official police business, but no one needed to know that. She'd signed out early, stating surveillance of a known felon as the cause. There was no designation for hunting for a potential witch on behalf of a homicidal being. Although they might have considered it a freelance gig, which was frowned upon.

The tall figure of Megan Armand popped up from behind the checkout counter. Her eyes flew open wide, and her mouth formed a perfect 'O' at the sight of Carmichael. Good. She was still intimidated by law enforcement, unlike her housemate.

"We just opened," said Megan. "I mean, I opened for Mlle. Georgette. She told me to. She called . . . I assume she got permission to call me from the prison. And she said to open up for her while she's away. That's not illegal, is it?"

Carmichael was pleased to see her so nervous, but also a little annoyed. She considered alleviating Megan's fears, but decided a little terror never hurt anyone. As long as Carmichael wasn't the one terrified.

Carmichael scowled, implying that running a criminal's shop was in itself a crime. Let the girl sweat it out. "We can discuss your boss later. I'm here to find the whereabouts of a Sabine Domingue. It is my understanding that the two of you live together in a home near the Greenwood Cemetery."

Megan Armand gaped like a grounded fish. Collecting herself, she snapped her mouth shut and shrugged in a poor pantomime of nonchalance. "I rarely know where Sabine is."

"You wouldn't mind my taking a look around here?"

"I, uhm, it's not my shop. I don't think I have the right to allow somebody to walk around. Not without a warrant. You don't have a warrant, do you?"

Carmichael considered lying. Instead, she raised her eyebrows and waited.

"It doesn't matter anyway. Sabine's not allowed in the shop. She and Georgette don't really get along and—"

Carmichael interrupted her. "Where did she go?"

"If you knew anything about Sabine, which I gather you do or you wouldn't be here looking for her, then you know there's no telling where she is and that's the God's honest truth. I haven't seen her in days."

"So, she's on the run?" Carmichael asked.

"On the run from what, exactly? Do you or don't you have a warrant?"

Carmichael ignored the question.

Megan was getting defensive, which wasn't helping. Carmichael checked herself. She needed to go a little easier, save her attitude for later, after she caught the little thief. She still hadn't decided whether to lock her away or 'remove' her by other means. Either way, it would do New Orleans a service to have that menace off the streets. And that was really the crux of her job as an NOPD detective, wasn't it?

"Does she have a job?" *Other than thieving the streets of New Orleans*, Carmichael decided not to say out loud. See, restraint was the key. This Megan was a simple person who required simple tactics.

"Sabine work?" A hint of a smile crossed Megan's lips. "Last I heard, she was considering going back to school."

Is she trying to toy with me?

"What school?"

Megan opened her mouth and stood like that for a moment too long. Carmichael was about to repeat her question just to get under the woman's skin when a thud upstairs drew both of their attention to the ceiling.

"Could that be her? Maybe she's attending class remotely." Carmichael smirked.

"No." Megan didn't elaborate, but her demeanor had gone from nervous and jumpy to fearful. Regretfully, it didn't seem like it was Carmichael that she was scared of.

"I think we need to take a look upstairs, don't you?" As Carmichael spoke, the electronic bell jingled behind her. Maybe this was going to be simpler than she thought. She swung around, hoping to catch Sabine entering. Instead, an older woman in an expensive but sensible pantsuit came through the door and looked around as if delighted.

"I have heard so much about your shop," she said with glee. "Benjamin told me about. Said it was cute as can be. Said if you want a gift, an authentic New Orleans memorabilia type gift to send to your nieces, this was the place to go. And it looks like he was right."

Megan and Carmichael froze, neither speaking as the woman tottered around, touching every crystal on her way past. Picking up each pack of tarot cards to examine before putting them back. Cooing at the Voodoo doll keychains. And finally ending up at the counter, inserting herself between Megan and Carmichael.

"Deary, if you're not too busy with this young lady." She cast a grandmotherly gaze at Carmichael and smiled sweetly before turning back to Megan. "Could you help me find something for my nieces?"

"I, uhm, Officer Carmin, right?" Megan said to Carmichael. Her expression was way too innocent for her to have made the mistake accidentally.

"Carmichael, Officer Carmichael." Getting angry at her wouldn't help, but Carmichael went ahead and got mad anyway.

The older woman looked abashed. Her hand fluttered about her chest. "Oh my. An officer. I didn't know. Without the uniform and all. And you being a woman, you know."

If the lady hadn't been so doddering, Carmichael would've suspected she was trying to get under Carmichael's skin. But the lady looked like one of the old-moneyed women of the French

Quarter. The kind that knew every official in the city and every donor as well. Hell, she probably donated a wing of the police station by the look of her.

The lady patted Carmichael's arm. "Sweetheart, I didn't mean to get in the way of your work. Is this an investigation? Don't tell me it's an investigation. I would just be so embarrassed if I were to get in the way of something important like an investigation."

Megan cleared her throat. "No ma'am. Officer Carlyle doesn't have business here. I believe she was just leaving. I am at your disposal."

Carmichael circled the shop three times, waiting for the older woman to choose her gifts and get out. No more suspicious thumps came from upstairs. She contemplated sneaking up, but Megan kept half an eye on her. Her nervousness had dispelled with the presence of the customer, who seemed determined to examine every single item in the shop.

Exasperated, Carmichael left.

She loitered in front of an antique shop one block away. Positioned behind a potted palm, she could observe who came and went from the front and back of the magic shop. No one did.

The older woman took her time shopping with no sign of Sabine or a fox coming or going. Carmichael's phone bleated for attention. It was a precinct phone number. She considered ignoring it, but thought better of it.

"Carmichael," she snapped.

On the other end, the superintendent launched into a long diatribe about more trouble at the French Market without bothering to identify herself first. Carmichael's jaw clenched and her shoulders tightened as she listened.

"I'll be right there," Carmichael said, then hung up and didn't budge from her spot behind the potted palm.

Chapter 18

MEGAN

Luckily, this sweet lady came in, giving Meg an excuse to dodge Carmichael. But Meg needed to get rid of both of them and get back upstairs. Not sure how to manage it, Meg followed the lady around trying to appear useful.

As she picked up one item after another, the lady told Meg that she was a lifelong resident of the French Quarter. She lived in a townhouse a few blocks away where she'd grown up, and apparently considered the surrounding area her domain. She was cheery, a little daft, but endearing, that was, until the shop door closed on Officer Carmichael.

As the annoying jingle of the door ceased, the slightly doddering older woman stood erect, shoulders squared, and faced Meg with a kind but authoritarian air.

"Keep an eye on the door, dear. I'll go upstairs and see how your guest is doing."

Meg stumbled over several excuses as to why no one was allowed in the private apartments when the woman raised a hand to shush her.

"Benjamin told you a Ms. Beauchamp would be here?"

Meg nodded, assuming she meant the older Creole man who helped the satyr.

"That would be me. He explained the situation after leading that poor boy here from the market. He'll be along shortly. He might have introduced himself as Ol' Ben, a name given to him long ago when he was still quite young. A good man, but we don't have time to exchange pleasantries. Just show him upstairs." Ms. Beauchamp gave Meg a level stare to be sure she understood her instructions.

Not knowing what to say, Meg gave her another curt nod.

"Very good," said Ms. Beauchamp, as if Meg had given the only correct answer. "Now go lock the front door and put up the closed sign. Then it'd be best if you checked the back, too. I'd bet my best blooming African violet that Officer Carmichael is staked out on the corner watching for you or your little witch friend to leave. We'll need to be sure she's occupied before we move our patient.

Meg didn't know how this lady had just transformed and neatly taken over the situation, but she did as she was told and looked out the front door. Carmichael headed up the block away from the river. She didn't look back over her shoulder, but Meg noticed the officer checking her reflection in the windows as she passed.

Clever. Meg was finally catching on to this amateur sleuthing. She doubted Sabine could've done better. In fact, Sabine probably would've just bitten Carmichael, possibly after changing into fox form, possibly not. And they'd all be sitting in jail with Mlle. Georgette.

"She's out of sight now up the street. I can't see if she stopped at the corner or not. Halfway up the stairs, there's another window, and we can see how far she's gotten." Meg followed Ms. Beauchamp to the back of the shop. It didn't speak well of her judgment that she trusted this stranger more than she trusted the cop. Or did it? Maybe it was because Carmichael seemed too eager to lock somebody up for something.

Meg and Beauchamp stop at the narrow window beside the stairwell. Meg peered out. "I don't see her."

Beauchamp looked around her shoulder. "There she is, trying her best to blend in with the potted palm outside Jeffrey's antique shop. It's amazing he can keep it looking so good without the full sun. You know they prefer full sun. I wonder if Benjamin had something to do with that."

Meg had no idea what this man Ben might have to do with a potted palm that needed sunlight, but she didn't ask. This was all too surreal. As if living with a witch and a crow and a goblin as a yard guest was not surreal.

"What do we do about her?" Meg fretted.

"We wait on Benjamin. We'll need him to help move the satyr. Now take me to the poor thing."

The satyr lay unconscious across an overturned coffee table in the middle of the living area. Well, that explained the crash.

After helping Ms. Beauchamp rouse the satyr and seat him on the settee, Meg went to lock the front door, only to find the older Creole man casually leaning against an iron post out front. He caught sight of her, flicked his cigarette to the curb, rubbed it out with the toe of his boot and sauntered over.

Meg opened the door. "Benjamin, right?"

He tipped his hat to her. "Ol' Ben will do just fine."

"Uh, well, Ms. Beauchamp said to head upstairs."

He gave her a wink and a smile and headed for the stairs while Meg locked the door, turned the sign to closed.

"Miss Beauchamp, I hear you're up here," Ol' Ben called up the stairs.

Ms. Beauchamp appeared at the top, hands on hips. "It's Lily, Benjamin, and you see I am. Get on up here. We gotta get this boy down and back to my place before I can be of much use to him."

"I figured as much. If anyone can help, you can." Benjamin climbed the stairs. His heavy leather boots silent on the old, creaky treads.

Living with a witch and a crow and a yard goblin had taught Meg that most unusual things were indeed unusual. No need to write them off. She followed, and every step loudly lamented her passage. She checked the street corner on her way by the window.

A large, dark-skinned man with a bald head and beefy arms had Carmichael's full attention. He was built like he once played high school football and now spent nights lifting weights. He wore a well-tailored gray suit over his muscular frame. His large hand rested gently on the officer's shoulder as he directed her into the antique shop. Carmichael shook her head, but the man led her inside, nonetheless.

Upstairs, Benjamin gently lifted the satyr off the settee. Beauchamp turned to Meg. "Does Jeffrey have our persistent policewoman in hand?"

So, the large man must be the antique shop owner that Ms. Beauchamp had mentioned earlier. The older residents of the French Quarter must have a tight-knit network. Meg laughed at how deftly they had handled Carmichael. "Yes, ma'am. I believe he does."

"Excellent. I'll go pull my car around and see if I can find an opening near the back."

"We'll wait for you downstairs, ma'am," Ol' Ben said respectfully.

Beauchamp shot Benjamin a look that said, even to Meg, that she did not approve of Benjamin calling her 'ma'am.' This was an odd pair. Meg immediately liked them.

Before Beauchamp could leave, Meg asked, "How did the two of you learn about satyrs and such?"

Benjamin started down the stairs without answering. Beauchamp patted her on the arm. "My dear, those are a series of stories that go back a lifetime for me, and Benjamin too, I expect. Maybe one day, when New Orleans is not in so much danger, we can sit down over a cup of coffee and share a story or two. Until then, we have other work to do."

With Carmichael still out of sight, Beauchamp pulled her Cadillac up to the sidewalk near the back entry to the shop long enough for Ol' Benjamin to carry the satyr out. Meg opened the car door, and the Creole man laid the unconscious creature across the back seat. Once the door was closed, the car took off like a jackrabbit.

Meg laughed again. Benjamin joined her this time.

"Miss Beauchamp, she's one-of-a-kind. You have a good day, miss." He tipped his hat to her again and sauntered down the sidewalk. As he passed the entry to the antique shop, he took a cigarette from a pocket in his shirt, paused to light it, then continued on toward Jackson Square.

"Well," Meg said to no one in particular. "What now?"

As if on cue, a figure stepped out from under the skeletal branches of a wisteria that draped across the fence, startling Meg.

"If you're done, come with me. We have a lot to do while those other two are occupied," said Warwick the goblin before he blended back into the shadows.

"Really?" Meg asked. "Because saving a satyr is not enough for one day."

But she followed. It's what she did.

Chapter 19

SABINE

A glowing object floated through trees silhouetted by the moon. At first, Sabine had mistaken it for a star, then it drifted closer, flashing on and off.

"A will-o'-the-wisp?" she asked, astounded by the magic pulsing off the glowing orb.

The young woman stood beside her, features lost in the shadows. "Hold out your hand."

The glowing orb came to her, lighting delicately upon her palm. Sabine curled her fingers around it, protecting it from the breeze.

"A firefly?" The luminescent insects had been magical to her as a child, but tonight, she was disappointed that it wasn't something more mysterious than an ordinary bug.

The older woman, now standing in the younger one's shoes, cackled.

Annoyed, Sabine opened her mouth for a sarcastic reply when the vicious bug bit her. Her fingers flew wide open, revealing a very grumpy looking sprite who glared up at her, teeth bared.

"That's just it, dear. Magic is all around you if you look close enough to figure out what it truly is. You're too busy making assumptions. Thinking you know something, when you barely know anything at all."

The sprite went in for another bite, but Sabine shook it off. It flew off glowing and grousing as it went.

"Your magic comes from that fire inside you. You been too busy stealing everyone else's to notice your own," the woman told her. Sabine couldn't tell in the gloom if it was the older or younger one speaking.

The next day, or maybe it had been more, Sabine sat on the steps of the cottage, elbows on knees, contemplating her way off the island. She'd learned nothing of consequence. Other than the two women holding her captive could change places suddenly and without notice.

As Sabine plotted, the darkness reached out from the tree shadows, blackened fingers grasping. She asked the older woman sitting in a rocker, "When do I get a pair of scissors of my own to snip the dark away?

"The scissors are mine. You're gonna have to learn how to cut your ties to the darkness in your own way."

The tips of the shadow fingers were only a hair's breadth from Sabine's fingertips when the familiar "Snip" sounded, clipping them off at the last minute before they latched on.

"Why does it come after me?" she asked. What she really meant was, "What is so dark in me that draws it like a magnet?" But she wouldn't say that out loud.

"There is no darkness in you." The young voice answered her unspoken question, but it was the older woman's that continued. "There's sadness. And sometimes that feels the same. You got nothing but fire in you. The dark is drawn to the light like a vine to the sun. But this darkness is looking to snuff out that fire of yours if it can. Don't let it."

"How do I keep it away if you won't give me a pair of scissors to cut it back?"

"Use what you got."

"Like my fingernails? My teeth?"

The young woman cackled, but it sounded a lot like the older one. The longer Sabine stayed, the harder time she had telling them apart.

Another afternoon, or maybe the same one, Sabine sat in the cozy kitchen at a worn wooden table with the woman snapping peas when a whip-like thread of darkness crept down the chimney, inched across the floorboards and up the table leg. It wormed its way through the pile of beans toward her hand.

Sabine held out her fingers, letting the tendrils wrap around them, then she took ahold and jerked. Which did not work *at all*. The darkness came in multiple threads, wrapping around her hands and wrists and pulling back. Sabine dug in her heels so it didn't drag her off the bench and up the chimney.

SNIP. SNIP. SNIP. The woman cut her free.

"Wrestling with it is definitely one way to go, but it's not the most effective, doesn't seem." The woman laughed and laughed. A great blue heron joined in, *croaking*.

Sabine stomped down the hall and shut herself inside the small bedroom assigned to her the first night. She flopped down on one of the two narrow twin beds and pouted. She would get out of here, and she would take those scissors with her. She had to save Thibodeaux from the darkness. And the market, she added belatedly, trying to convince herself the detective wasn't her only concern.

When had she started thinking of him as Thibodeaux again instead of Jean-Luc? Probably when he agreed to partner with her on a beautiful vengeance plot over croissants, then shoved her aside before she'd even digested them. It didn't matter. It was the market and Baylur and Georgette she was concerned with. Not what the detective was up to. That time, she almost believed herself.

Thibodeaux wasn't the only one to discredit her abilities. The Voodoo priestesses must have sent her here believing she'd learn how to deal with her magic. They acted as if they were afraid Sabine, as is, would be a hindrance if the darkness broke free at the market. But this woman sitting in the middle of the bayou didn't seem too concerned about anything back in the city. All her attention seemed to be focused on torturing Sabine, rather than on teaching her.

"I'm teaching, child," the woman had said. "You're just not listening."

There'd been other attempts at lessons, about pulling up the glow from inside. Lessons about pushing it back down. All fuzzy in Sabine's memory. None of it useful. But she did learn a thing or two.

She learned the house sat in the middle of a floating island. It drifted across the bayou, and every few days it would bump into the shore. When the house jolted and the trees quivered, that meant it had connected with land. Sabine kept alert to these tiny vibrations. She studied the quickest path from the house to the water's edge, where the alligator waited. She was sure it was the same one with its haughty expression and toothy smile. It kept a careful eye on her, and she on it as she picked up another tidbit of information.

Sabine could tell by the direction of the ripples on the water which side of the island had connected. She had yet to make it to the shore before the island floated away again. But she would. She just hoped she made it back to New Orleans before the darkness burst through from the market, setting loose all manner of creatures on its unsuspecting citizens.

Chapter 20

WARWICK

As the air cooled, fog rolled in off the river and crept down the streets, seeking lost souls. Although the dense air shielded Megan from fellow pedestrians, it did nothing for Warwick, who needed no more than a tree shadow in which to hide.

"You will get home," Warwick assured himself, but he could not traverse the barrier to the Beyond alone. His banishment from Philip's goblin court had allowed him into the In Between, but no further. Since the market evicted him, he had to seek an unguarded entrance. That is where he led Megan Armand, who had the inhuman ability to traverse realms at will.

"What did you say?" Megan laid a hand on his shoulder and leaned in close to listen.

Warwick forced himself not to jerk her hand away. "We're getting close. Do you feel the draw of the Beyond?"

"Can you sense the dead?" Her grip tightened on his jacket, making his skin crawl. These humans had an inordinate need to touch. However, her proximity caused the fog to split and flow around them.

Warwick did not answer. You cannot walk the streets of this city without feeling the surrounding dead. They walked past a row of houses, windows shuttered. In that silence, he realized only the dead in their proximity were asleep. Odd.

Megan released him, straightened his collar where she had rumpled it, and resumed her nervous chatter. "You didn't mean Heaven or Hell when you said the Beyond, did you?"

Again, he refused to answer her needless questions.

That did not deter her. "Stupid of me. Of course you didn't. You're talking about your home. I'm sorry."

"The Beyond is not my home. The Beyond is a word you simple creatures use to describe everything beyond your realm. I come from the great Court of Philip the First, King and ruler of the Goblin Realm." A stone knotted behind his breastbone as he said the name. He accepted the pain as penance.

As if she could feel it too, Megan looked at him with pity. How dare she? Then, a most horrendous catastrophe befell him. Megan Armand wrapped her long arm around his shoulders and hugged him tight against her side.

"Whatever you call it, we will get you back there, Warwick. I promise."

Unable to restrain himself, Warwick shrugged off her embrace. He had just informed her he was of the Court of King Philip, and yet she still took liberties with his person. Unthinkable!

"Here we are," she said, oblivious to her insult.

The sun was well down by the time they approached the tall walls, keeping the living from the dead.

"How do you know it's in St. Louis Cemetery?" she asked. "They're a lot of cemeteries in New Orleans. There are even two St. Louis. This is No. 1."

"I don't go by numbers. You should be able to feel it. This is the oldest dwelling place of the dead. Of your dead. I sense there are others much older. But they have been desecrated by your buildings. So we shall start here."

A crumbling brick wall ran alongside the walk. At its center stood an iron gate. Warwick stepped back and motioned for Megan to open it.

"Can't you do whatever you need from out here?"

"The passage is within these walls. Please open the gate." Stating the obvious had become tedious, but Warwick was learning it was necessary.

"We can't just go in. It's locked at night. I don't think they run tours this late."

"Best if we do not have any more of your kind around."

"My kind? Don't you think that's a little condescending?"

If he had successfully kept it to only a *little* condescending, then he was doing exceedingly well. "Please, as I asked, open the gate."

"It is locked. We cannot go in. It's illegal." Megan spoke to him in slow, segmented phrases, as if he could not understand her.

Ignore her ignorance, he told himself. Megan Armand means well. He shook his head and waggled his fingers at the lock. "Do the thing you humans do when a door is locked. Like the petite thief does."

"Do you think all of us are trained at lock picking? We're not all thieves."

He snorted at the suggestion. "If you lack the necessary skills, we shall have to go over the wall. Although I am the stronger of the two, you are the longest of limb. Scamper to the top and offer me a hand." He bowed graciously and waved for her to ascend.

"I'm not a squirrel. I don't scamper. And it's illegal. You do understand that part, right? Or is that why you got kicked out of the market?"

Megan's growing confidence was becoming a nuisance.

"You live with a thief. You broke into Mlle. Georgette's shop of magic. I do not believe you have the moral standing to scoff at my suggestion. Do you?"

"I didn't break in. And Sabine . . . Is just Sabine."

They glared at one another for several heartbeats as the mists found their way around and in between the two of them, seeking to divide their forces. Again, Warwick felt the plucking at the edges of his garments. Just as he feared, he would have to break the stalemate and convince her of the worthiness of his cause, which even he knew was dubious, she relented.

"Fine. Since you're the strongest, give me a boost."

He didn't react immediately as she pantomimed weaving her fingers together to create a stirrup. He sighed. Though it was beneath his dignity, his need was greater than his pride. He went to one knee and offered her this *boost*.

Once inside, they crept between the houses of the dead, and Megan's nervous chatter resumed. "It's funny how little space we take up in death and how much in life."

You have not seen the halls of the Goblin Realm, he thought wistfully.

"How do you know where to go?" Megan asked, following him down a sleepy alley, between two crypts, and alongside a columbarium.

"If you cannot feel it, there is no point in my explaining." His words seemed to agitate her, which had the effect of dulling her fear. He did not know if that was a good development or not.

"You really are arrogant. Sabine was right about that. And she would know about arrogance."

He had a right to be, so there was no reason to respond. Megan's footsteps crackled across weathered leaves. The walls kept the fog from entering too quickly, but they only posed a temporary deterrent. Down the long alley, threads of mist crept through the gates. Interesting that humans believed the walls could keep the dead bound.

A melancholy musical note pierced the quiet. A sliding crescendo followed. Music wafted through the air, driving back the fog.

"What's that?" Megan grabbed his arm.

Warwick wrenched it away. "You can hear it? How interesting. I was beginning to believe you had no sense at all."

"Where is it coming from?" Megan asked as the music wrapped around them and reverberated off the concrete walls. The echo bounced between concrete crypts.

"That would be my fellow musicians." A voice floated up to them. "Sounds like I'm running late for tonight's gig. Excuse me if you will." An icy breeze brushed past them and split the fog on its way to a whitewashed monolith set against the outer wall of the cemetery.

"You heard that right?" Megan asked, moving quickly from nervous to fearful.

Anything out of the normal threw these creatures into a tantrum.

"Come along. It may know where the portal to the Beyond lies."

"That's what you wanted? We could've gone to the Midnight Jazz Club for that. Why the cemetery?"

"This one is not so heavily guarded." Warwick followed the music. It grew louder as they approached the crypt. A plaque on the side read, 'The New Orleans Musicians' Tomb.'

"Oh, I've heard about The Musicians' Tomb." This seemed to comfort her.

The music soared around them. The souls of each instrument played a different song, yet they merged together, composing a litany of the dead. As the song came to an end with the slide of notes, a translucent face formed in front of the crypt. A body filled in beneath it.

"What brings you two wanderers into the cemetery tonight?"

"Why are so few of you awake this evening?" Warwick asked. He would need to avoid notice, even from the dead, if necessary. If they remain asleep, that would be the best scenario. And they could leave this quartet behind once he had directions to the Beyond.

"I'd say most of us are awake. I'm the first back. Although those lazybones stayed behind 'til it was time to play. Most of us answered the Voodoo priestesses when they called. Unusual to have a gathering that big. But they had questions, and we gave what answers we could. They show us respect, we show them respect.

"Now I'll ask again. What y'all doing in here at night? Unless you came to hear us play. I'm guessing you didn't since I can still hear your heart beating like a big ol' bass drum." The apparition said, looking at Warwick. Then he turned a benevolent smile on Megan. "Yours, my dear, is more snare drum. You needn't fear me. But you might want to clear out before the rest return. Some are pretty ornery."

Megan squeaked. Gulped. Then spoke. "That sounds like good advice. Come on, Warwick," she said. "We need to go."

"We will go when I get answers. You gave answers to the priestesses, you can give answers to me."

"Now, that don't sound too respectful to me. Does it to you, boys?"

A trumpet let loose a *"BLAT"* followed by gravely laughter.

Megan yelped and made to run, but met with another wraith at her back.

"Not so fast, Missy. Your fella here's got something to say. And I'd like to hear it."

Warwick squared his shoulders, lifted his chin, and spoke in a commanding tone to the spirits. "Show me your portal to the Beyond."

A rattle like that of old bones thrown across the head of a drum tumbled around them. Warwick did not flinch, though the tall one looked as if she would fold in upon herself. He repeated his demand.

"If we had a path to the Great Beyond, don't you think we'd be there?" a spirit said in a deep but melodious voice.

Megan cleared her throat and spoke in a much squeakier voice. "He doesn't mean *that* Beyond. He's not talking about death." Her final word came out as a whisper barely heard over the breeze stirring the fog.

Warwick repeated himself using the language of his people. "Show me the way to the Beyond."

The whisper of the wind stilled. The hum of vibrating strings and echo of notes lingering in the air all hushed. The wraiths parted and faded between crypts.

"I said, Show Me!" Warwick's words fell flat on the houses of the dead.

Megan gently touched his shoulder and whispered. "I think they're gone."

He stiffened under her touch, refusing to leave, when a wavering in the air drew his attention. It swelled before him, floated between him and the tall one on its way toward an alley leading back to the cemetery wall. He followed, and it dissipated in front of a door hanging akimbo on rusted hinges in a pointed stone arch.

"Enter." The word reverberated in his head. The word that his people used for the lands on the other side.

"Come," he called to Megan, who hung back, eyes wide with terror.

"Not in there."

"Quick now, before the opening moves again. I need you. I cannot enter the Beyond alone. Not anymore."

Chapter 21

THIBODEAUX

Stragglers left the French Market as the sun set, loaded down with unmarked boxes. Their movements predatory. Their gaze feral. Even this late at night, the tourists used to still be lively and ready for a night on the town. This crew kept hands inside their coats as if close to weapons. Their eyes darted back-and-forth searching for prey while trying not to be preyed upon.

Instead of sequined masks and lacquered paintings, booths now held inconspicuous brown paper bags or carved masks, appearing monstrous and animated in the shadows.

Jean-Luc walked down one side of the market to Jackson Square and back up the other side.

As day turned to night, the homeless huddled in doorways, under blankets, and next to their dogs. Vendors packed their wares as the fog rolled through the opening in the river wall and under the pavilion roof.

Jean-Luc had spent another day searching for any sign of Sabine. When she was on the hunt, she could be virtually invisible. He wouldn't worry, but she hadn't spoken to him since the morning they all met in her kitchen. They'd parted with her mad and determined to get into trouble.

Before that meeting, the two of them had hashed out a plan over coffee and croissants in the morning mist. A dirty but delightful plot to lure that blue fae bastard over and take him and Georgette out of the equation. A month earlier than that, and she wouldn't have trusted him with such a plan.

Then he'd told her to stay out of it. That he'd take care of it. It was too dangerous for her when she had such little control over magic. Warwick had been right. The market was about to burst from within, and monsters were on the loose.

And one of them is you, he told himself, but shoved the thought aside.

The petite thief should have surfaced by now. Even while sulking, she would have taken time to complain to Megan about the flavor of ice cream in the freezer or the staleness of their croissants. But Megan was camped out with that creature at Georgette's and said she hadn't seen Sabine.

Sabine's absence provided the perfect excuse to return to the market. Jean-Luc had promised himself to stay away after he overreacted, dislocating a young man's shoulder, but his resolve hadn't lasted a full forty-eight hours. He tried, knowing Sabine was right. It's where he wanted to be.

Warwick had called them all out for it. A part of Jean-Luc was glad it wasn't just him. They were all drawn to the market. But none of them carried the darkness inside like he did.

After walking laps up and down the length of the pavilion, he had to admit she wasn't there. Or she didn't want to see him. Either way, he had no excuse left for being at the market.

Unless . . .

Unless he could find an ally here among the monsters. Someone, or something, willing and able to help guard his city.

Emboldened by the fog coverage rolling in, Jean-Luc stepped into the deserted market.

It thrummed with dark energy even after the black scar at its center had healed. Shortly before Mardi Gras, a black cloud had burst through from the Beyond then disappeared leaving a scorched area behind. The concrete had been patched, and the roof repaired. Jean-Luc had hoped the malicious intent would leave as well. Instead, it had stayed and festered, infecting those human vendors who returned.

As he entered the market, a hulking figure with a massive head and matching shoulders circled the pavilion. The bullheaded creature spotted Jean-Luc and headed his way, its hooves striking the concrete. The detective had seen it once before, chasing Sabine last fall. It stopped at the market's center and faced him, knees bent, as if preparing to charge.

Jean-Luc raised his voice to carry the thirty yards between them. "If I understand correctly, you're the one in charge of protecting the Faerie Market from intruders, criminals, and troublemakers. Not doing so well lately. Are you?"

The beast snorted. Its hoof scraped the concrete.

"It's my job to protect the market on this side. I've been doing a pretty crappy job, too," he called, then steeled himself, bracing for impact, but the creature stood its ground. So the detective continued. "The way I see it, we have the same objective."

The beast sneered.

"Going forward, if you need my help, I'll be there if I'm able."

It snorted again without moving, and a bank of fog rolled between the two of them. When it dissipated, the creature was gone.

Well, that was the best Jean-Luc could expect. He'd made his offer, and the beast hadn't gored him. Maybe, just maybe, it understood. Now, what Jean-Luc could do to help, that was the question. But making monstrous alliances seemed a good idea when dealing with monstrous problems.

He left, knowing he'd be back, but maybe he'd have help if that creature had the moral code of a cop aiding a cop.

The market dragged at his shadows, attempting to hold him captive, but Jean-Luc refused to be trapped ever again. Fighting the pull, he made it out and headed up Decatur.

As he passed the first lamppost, he heard his name.

"Detective Jean-Luc Thibodeaux." It wasn't a question. A woman of color with russet-colored hair gave him half a smile, bringing out a dimple in her cheek. "Fancy seeing you walking about this late at night. What you looking for?"

"Just checking to make sure there's no trouble down here," he nodded and was about to take off when she flicked a finger to stop him.

"You come to stop the trouble, to start it, or to join it?"

"What's that?" Jean-Luc felt the darkness rising within him. He kept it down while he was in the pavilion, but a tendril crossed his left eye before he could blink it away.

She grinned a wicked grin. "Ahh, there it is. I suspected you had the dark on you. Agnes said no. She always thinks the best of everyone, but she prepares for the worst. I'll give her that. Sissy says you need help. I'm not sure there's much we can do for you." She looked him up and down like he was a degenerate, coming into her living room, tracking mud on her carpet.

"Excuse me, ma'am. Do we know one another?"

"We know about you. And we know there's a darkness on the market. What we don't know is how much the two go together. We've been doing what we can to hold it back. Time you do your part."

"And you are?"

"Priestess Makayla," she scowled at him as if he should've known.

Jean-Luc gave a slight bow in acknowledgment of the Voodoo priestess's status. "Priestess Makayla, we appreciate all the help you and yours can offer. Can I help you get where you're going this evening?"

"I can help myself. Thank you very much."

"Well, thank you again for your help. You have a good night and stay safe on the streets." With another nod, he headed off down Decatur, thinking Wilhelm had been right about the priestesses keeping an eye on things.

He hadn't made it more than a step or two before he heard his name again. The priestess spoke in a goading tone. "Maybe you can concentrate on doing your work now that that little fox is out of your way."

"What's that?" Jean-Luc swung around, but she was already headed down the street. "You know where Sabine is? Is she okay?"

The priestess spoke over her shoulder without stopping. "Oh, I expect she'll get what's coming to her. About time the little menace got taken care of."

"Where is she?"

The woman flipped her hand and didn't even turn her head this time, so he could barely make out her words. "Oh, I expect the little fox is out running in the bayou somewhere. Hope an alligator don't find her."

She chuckled to herself, and Jean-Luc had to restrain himself from running after her to wrench every bit of information out of her.

"*Craaw. Craaw.*" A crow called from the night sky, then swooped down to land atop the lamppost.

"Bertrand?" he asked, knowing the answer.

"Cr-r-r-uck."

"I know. I know." Jean-Luc grimaced. "But I'm listening now. Where is she?"

Chapter 22

MEGAN

W hat would you have us do here?" Meg asked Warwick. She wrapped her arms tight around herself, though the air wasn't chilled on this side of the tomb. It ought to be. She had the terrible urge to check the charms on her bracelet to see if she had been in this part of the Beyond before, but she knew she hadn't.

A stone bridge stretched from the tomb behind them across a chasm and into the rocky landscape beyond. She looked over the edge. A mistake. There appeared to be no bottom.

"If we move with haste, we should catch up with the market before it moves again," the goblin said irritably.

"Why is it you need me in this place?" Meg looked about for the fae Baylur. She feared if she lingered in the Beyond too long, he would know and come for her. She didn't know if she had the strength to escape him again. At least this time Warwick knew where she was. She hoped he cared enough to help if she was abducted.

"I have not been able to access the Beyond since I was expelled from the market. Even it no longer welcomes me on the quarter moon."

"Why can't you access it from the Midnight Jazz Club? Who's guarding it there?"

"Powers you wouldn't understand."

"You might be surprised," she said defensively.

Warwick snorted.

"There are other waypoints that aren't in cemeteries," she pointed out. Regretfully, she remembered using one of them now that she had her charm bracelet back.

"The others have not permitted my passage. I did not know until we tried if this one would or not, even with you."

"Why me?" Meg rubbed a thumb across the charms of her bracelet, feeling memories dart around inside her head. She jerked her hand back before her mind seized on one.

"You are gifted, Megan Armand. The Beyond allows you to come and go at will as if you are one of its own."

"But I am not. There is not a magical bone in my body. Is this because of the bracelet?"

"If that were the enchantment on the bracelet, I would not have so easily given it away."

Meg wasn't sure if it was an enchantment. Really more of a curse. She would've been happy to stay in her world and know next to nothing about magic, no more than a local psychic could offer. She could live without that, too. But those days were gone.

"Well, you're here now. Can I go back?"

"I bid you to stay with me. Lest I need your aid to get back."

"Do you want to go back? I always kind of thought you were homesick."

Warwick did not answer but started across the bridge. Meg looked back at the empty tomb, down to the empty abyss, and forward to the receding figure of the gnarled goblin.

"Wait up. If you want to come back and live in Sabine's shed, who am I to judge?"

"It would be best for the two of us to move quietly. There are those who would want to know of our presence here. And they do not wish us well."

Goosebumps lined Meg's arms. Great.

The far side of the bridge never seemed more than a few yards away yet never grew any closer. The goblin knew Baylur would be looking for her. Yet Warwick still asked her to come. This must be important to him.

"Why don't they want you here?"

Without looking back to see if she followed, Warwick stepped from the bridge into the long moon shadows of tall, leafless trees. From one step to the next, he disappeared and reappeared. Afraid of losing sight of him for good. Meg jogged to catch up. She walked close enough that their arms brushed against one another. She found it comforting.

As they walked through the forest, the moon set, the sun rose and was on its way down again. Meg had lost months here before in the matter of days back in New Orleans. She wondered if Sabine would try to come and find her this time.

She wondered if *she* needed to go looking for *Sabine*.

It was not unusual for the fox to disappear before dark and reappear just after dawn. Sometimes they would go a day or so without seeing one another. But not a week. Meg decided when she got back she needed to figure out what had happened to her housemate. Perhaps Warwick and Thibodeaux would help.

Blisters swelled and tore on the bottoms of her feet, and they continued to walk. She grew tired and would've fallen behind if the goblin's stride wasn't so much shorter than hers. They were still deep in the forest, and the moon had yet to rise a second time. She could barely see the goblin beside her.

"Is it much further?"

"Shhhh."

The clanging of brass bells reached her ears as the barren trees thinned out. By the time they reached the edge of the dead forest, Meg could also hear guttural voices raised in argument. Warwick raised a hand, signaling for her to halt. Meg stopped beside a tree almost big enough around to hide behind. She placed a hand against the bark and leaned around to watch the goblin exit the forest.

Although she hadn't seen their light while in the trees, pavilions now sprouted up across a burnt field. Torches lit booths with silhouetted figures fighting like a murmur's tale. It looked like an ancient puppet show depicting the terrors of hell. She shrank behind the trunk as Warwick boldly walked into the midst of the fighting creatures.

Something like sap, slow and sticky, ran over her fingers. She snatched them away and scraped her hand on the bark. It came away with strands connecting her fingers to the tree, and a centipede the size of her forearm fell to the ground. She jumped away from the trunk and scrubbed her hand against her jeans before realizing she was fully exposed to the creatures in the field.

Moving slowly, mouth agape, she raised her head to see if the beasts had noticed her. The shadowed market lit by firelight was gone, leaving the tinkling of silver bells and fairy globes bobbing invitingly over tables covered in silks and satin. Cheery faces greeted customers. All types of creatures with children in tow wandered from booth to booth, laughing.

Warwick was nowhere to be seen.

"So, which one is the real market and which is an illusion?" Meg asked the trees' shadows. She should probably keep quiet, but speaking out loud helped dispel the hellish image of the monstrous market from her mind's eye.

Sticking close to the tree line, she eased into the field and squinted to see what lay past this brighter market. Holding her hand up against the light, she began to make out distant mountains against a tapestry of stars. The moon rose, its light glistening on snow-covered peaks.

Was that where the ice giants lived?

Meg considered checking the charms on her bracelet to see if she could remember the shape of the mountains where the king of the ice giants ruled, but thought better of it. In this changing landscape, it would be best for her not to lose herself in a memory.

Despite her wariness, Meg's eyes began to droop, and she fought back a yawn. She sank to the ground, partially hidden by the tall grass, and watched for Warwick to reappear, unsure what she would do if he didn't.

As she waited, a great shadow blotted out the moon. A cry echoed across the fields. The bright market winked out. Meg held her breath and listened in the silence that followed.

Just past the thudding of her heartbeat, she thought she heard the crackle of footsteps coming up the slope beside her. The air against her arm shifted. She felt rather than saw her breath mist in front of her. She felt the air shudder as if a cold hand reached for her when the moon reappeared.

Warwick approached from the center of the burnt field, still several yards away. She cut her eyes as far as she could without turning her head to see if someone was beside her. Warwick looked over her shoulder as he came closer, but looked away as if he had seen nothing.

But what had made him look?

Without speaking, he waved for her to stand and follow. Once in the trees, she looked back to see if anyone was stalking them. No one did, but the flicker of torchlight and the dance of angry shadows played again across the field.

They walked back in silence through the forest, their exit much faster than their entrance. This time, the far side across the bridge was only a stone's throw away.

At the entrance to the tomb, Meg caught at Warwick's sleeve. "Did you find what you wanted?"

The goblin's shoulders slumped. His chin bowed nearly to his chest. He shook his head, then looked up at her, his eyes filled with sorrow. "No, but I found what we needed." He pulled out of her grasp and stepped into the tomb.

Meg called after him. "Warwick, thanks for coming back. I was afraid you might choose to stay at the market."

She could barely hear his response as he entered the dark tomb. But she thought he said, "It would not let me."

A chill rose at her back, and an imagined hand reached for her. This time, Meg did not look back. She just ran in after the goblin.

Chapter 23

SABINE

The light trickled in through white eyelet curtains. Sabine woke without remembering going to sleep. She and the elderly woman, or had it been the younger one, had talked through the day and into the night. And the pattern repeated. Scraps of the conversation still floated through her consciousness. Others fluttered away like a breeze crossing over a field of butterflies. She still wasn't sure that this was not a piece of the Beyond. She might have been on the island for days or maybe weeks. Surely not months.

She remembered finally asking the woman in exasperation, "If I have magic, how come I don't know how to use it?"

The woman answered in plain language, no riddles, and Sabine had seemed to understand her at the time, but lying here under the patchwork quilt with cicadas buzzing outside, she couldn't remember a word of it.

This morning, she lay still on top of the quilt. She was dressed with her slippered feet hanging off the edge of the bed. As irritating as the woman might be, the place felt too much like home for Sabine to put her muddy slippers on the bedspread. She lay still with her hands folded on her chest and held her breath, waiting.

It felt like it was time for the island to make landfall. She couldn't tell how it was she knew, but she did. And there it was. Cypress fronds rained down from the tree branches. The house quivered. The glass rattled in the old wooden window frame, which Sabine had left open through the night. She slipped her hand under the pillow.

Yes. The scissors were still there from the night before. She'd taken to stealing them at night and returning them in the morning before the older woman woke. Stuffing them in her satchel, she pulled the strap over her head, fell into fox form, and leapt out the window.

Reaching the water's edge, Sabine found the direction of the ripples and ran counterclockwise around the island until she found where one piece of land touched the other. As she launched herself into the air, a cackle sounded from every direction at once, and a tug at her satchel knocked her from the air and dragged her back onto the island.

She dug her claws into the loamy soil. The strap of the satchel dug into her shoulder as she scrambled to gain ground. She considered ducking out of the strap, but the scissors were in the bag. Crouching low and bunching her muscles, she put her weight against the strap and the tension broke, launching her nose first into the damp earth on the opposite shore. Regaining her feet, or paws, she sprinted away as the island broke free and floated away.

As it receded, the young woman's voice spoke softly in her ear. "See you back soon."

Ignoring the spooky voice, Sabine ran, dodging around pines and magnolias, and over downed trees until she found an old dirt road. She headed straight down the middle and nearly ran into an old dark blue sedan. It skidded to a halt, leaving ruts in the road.

Stunned, she jumped and landed on the hood rather than be smashed against the grill. She fell onto her haunches, nose pressed against the glass, staring at a familiar man with a look of horror and his eyes. She made ready to leap into the woods at the side of the road when the door burst open.

"Sabine!" Thibodeaux climbed out of the car and threw himself between her and the trees.

Arresting her jump, Sabine fell to the dirt on all fours in human form. Climbing to her feet, she dusted off her skinned knees and looked up into the shocked face of the detective.

"What are you doing out here?" She scowled at him. It was Thibodeaux, but he was definitely not himself. He hadn't shaved in days, and his eyes were dark, even though she didn't see the telltale black tendrils.

"Looking for you," he said.

"How'd you know where to look?"

"I didn't. All I knew was the bayou. But Bertrand helped."

"Creakee!" Bertrand squawked and landed on the open car door.

"About time," Sabine told the crow.

"You're welcome, again," he said in his rusty voice

Ignoring the smartass crow talk, Sabine told Thibodeaux, "Get me outta here."

Cackling echoed from both sides of the road, from above and from behind. Thibodeaux waved toward the open driver's door. Bertrand launched into the air and headed back the way the car had come. Sabine dove in and scrambled over the stick shift and into the passenger seat while Thibodeaux climbed in after her, no questions asked.

He just slammed the door, rammed the car into drive, and skidded into a three-point turn.

Sabine slouched down in the seat and heaved a sigh of relief.

"Buckle up," he said, clicking his own belt as he sped down the road.

"Really?" she asked.

"Really."

Once they reached the blacktop and turned back towards the highway, Sabine asked, "Why'd you come out here looking for me?"

"You went missing without telling anyone where you'd gone. What did you expect me to do?"

"Not that," she said in a near whisper.

His knuckles were white as he gripped the steering wheel. A muscle in his jaw clicked as he clenched it. Sabine thought she saw black tendrils cross the whites of his eyes before he blinked them away.

They drove in silence until I-55 turned into I-10, leading into New Orleans. Then the conversation started up again haltingly.

"How did you even know where to start looking?"

"I didn't at first. One of the Voodoo priestesses just said you were out in the bayou. You know how many bayous there are around here? But I asked one and then another until I got to one who said she thought it had been long enough and pointed me in the right direction. I thought I was going to have to start locking people up to get answers."

"Can you do that?"

"Not anymore. Not at all, really. Not just to get answers for where one thief/witch/fox might be hiding in the bayou."

"I wasn't hiding. I was kidnapped."

He had the audacity to snort. She punched him on the arm. "Ow! It's just hard to imagine anyone keeping you against your will."

She snorted at that. "True, but she had me . . . confused."

He cut his eyes over to her, then back to the road. "Did you learn anything?"

"I didn't need to learn anything."

"So, nothing then."

She considered punching him again, but held off for fear he might think it was a sign of affection. Instead, she brought up an old grievance. Well, not old, but the one they'd ended on.

"You were quick to set me aside along with the Georgette vengeance plan, weren't you? Thought you'd go after Baylur on your own, cut me out," Sabine accused while looking out the window to keep from meeting his eyes. He didn't reply, even with a grunt.

It took a minute or two of getting off the interstate, driving down the road towards her aunt's house—her house—before he spoke. "I was worried with the market getting worse. If it's not cleaned up soon, it's going to erupt into New Orleans."

"Quarter moon, when's that?" Sabine had lost all perception of time while trapped on the island.

"Tomorrow."

"Shit."

"Yep."

"And you're out here looking for me?"

"Yeah," Thibodeaux said. Sabine couldn't read his expression. They sat in an awkward silence as he turned off Canal Street. She knew the market was a bigger issue than Georgette and Baylur, and still Jean-Luc had taken time to come look for her.

But he still hadn't answered for reneging on their deal. And she wasn't done being sore about it.

"So, you're not going after Baylur anymore. And you expect me to what? Forget about him and Georgette? Because I'm not going to."

"I didn't say we were forgetting about them."

"Oh, so it's *we* again?"

"It always was." His voice was gruff.

"Didn't sound like it." Hers was sullen.

His tone shifted to something warm and private. "I just wanted you safe."

"I can keep *myself* safe."

"I know."

Well, what was she supposed to say to that? She couldn't decide if she wanted to be irritated or comforted, so she remained silent.

Jean-Luc cleared his throat. "Since we're co-conspirators again, I thought I might run a new plan by you, whereby we take care of the market when it shows back up and dispatch the demonic duo at the same time.

"What you got in mind?"

"We've been handed an opportunity to improve upon our original plan, which lacked some . . . finesse. Blunt and effective, maybe, but you and I both understood we probably wouldn't come out clean on the other side."

Sabine snorted. Her conscience would've been clear. She figured the witch and fae had it coming, but Sabine worried about the hold the dark already had on Jean-Luc. With that terminal integrity of his, taking out the two might be enough to give it full control of him.

"So who handed you this elegant plan?"

"Megan. Georgette wants her help to break out of prison."

"She didn't say anything about that in our little family meeting."

"Georgette called again." Thibodeaux cut his eyes at her. "I'm not sure if Megan would have fessed up to the scheme if I hadn't been there to intercept the call. Megan thinks if Georgette gets out, she's headed to the market where she'll flee into the Beyond, and Baylur will take care of her."

"Yeah, after he dumped her like a rotten fish the first time?"

"Oh, now," Thibodeaux said with a sly smile. "Don't underestimate the power of true love to conquer all."

She gave him the side-eye, and he gave a dark laugh.

"All right," Sabine said begrudgingly. "I'm listening."

Chapter 24

THIBODEAUX

Jean-Luc followed Sabine through the dimly lit house. Neither of them turned on lights until they reached the kitchen. This was the first time he'd been alone with her in the witch's cottage. Without the others, it seemed oddly intimate.

Last fall, Jean-Luc had cleaned up the murder scene. At the time, Sabine had been holed up in the attic of an abandoned townhouse in the Quarter after her aunt's murder. When Jean-Luc discovered no one had bothered to scrub the blood from the floors or repair the bullet holes in the cabinet, he'd taken it upon himself. He hadn't told Sabine what he'd done, but he knew she suspected.

Megan had probably guessed and made sure to tell her housemate. The two women had run here to hide when Georgette was still on the loose. He was glad they weren't greeted with a house of horrors, that he'd gotten there first.

Sabine was such a tiny, mighty creature full of fire and fear. He'd been so afraid for her out in the bayou. Now, watching her, face scrunched in determination, hiding that fear while she scrounged in the wrong cabinet for coffee filters, he had the sudden urge to wrap her in his arms and comfort her.

She'd probably bite.

He crossed his arms and resisted the urge to tell her he'd put them in the far left drawer when he stocked the kitchen. He leaned against the counter and watched as she carefully filled the carafe and started the pot. Her mouth formed a flat line. Her eyes narrowed.

Was she thinking of what happened on that island? Was she wondering why it had taken him so long to come and look?

Jean-Luc searched for the words to excuse the delay in looking for her. There were none. He had been preoccupied by the market. That was the shameful truth. Deep down, he also knew he'd never have found her without Bertrand's aid. If Jean-Luc had listened to the crow when it first came to him in the market, begging the detective to help her . . . but he hadn't. He'd been focused on his revenge plan even after telling her to drop hers.

He opened his mouth to apologize when the front door slammed, and Megan shouted from the living room.

"I thought you were going straight to the shed to sulk."

A black streak soared down the hallway to the kitchen and landed in the middle of the table. Sabine and Jean-Luc had left the crow perched on the front pediment, presumably guarding the door. Megan Armand followed Bertrand into the kitchen and startled at the sight of them. "Oh, I thought you were—"

She cut herself off as she dove at Sabine and snatched her into a hug. The petite thief wriggled but didn't bite. Jean-Luc couldn't help but wish he were the one hugging her instead.

"Enough." Sabine's words were muffled against Megan's side.

Her housemate held Sabine at arm's length, examining her. "When did you get back?" Without waiting for an answer,

Megan turned to Jean-Luc. "You found her, didn't you? I knew you would."

Then, suddenly, he found himself enveloped in a hug from the tall woman. The wrong woman, but he hugged her back, nonetheless, if only in gratitude for believing in him when he didn't.

"Where's the grumpy one?" Sabine asked, looking in the wrong cabinet for coffee mugs. Jean-Luc pointed to the right one, but before he could catch her attention, Megan pushed Sabine aside and retrieved four mismatched cups.

"You mean other than you?" Megan laughed, obviously delighted at the reappearance of her housemate, but her eyes were wild and her laughter too brittle. "He's out in the shed. Or that's where he said he was going. I asked him to come in. Somehow, he beat me back here from the—"

Megan cut herself off.

Starting again, she said, "Well, he wouldn't ride with me from the shop. But he was standing on the sidewalk when I got here, like he was afraid I wouldn't make it home. But I did. And you did. I'm so glad you're back." Megan tried for another hug, but Sabine held a mug up between them as a shield.

"Should we get him?" Sabine asked Jean-Luc?

"He's had a hard night. Let him be," Megan said, then eyed Sabine. "Instead, why don't *you* start by telling us where you've been?"

Sabine climbed onto the counter with a fresh cup of coffee and held out another to Jean-Luc. With her back to Megan, Sabine's eyes were wide, questioning how to respond. They'd agreed to keep their side plan between the two of them. No need to incriminate Megan. And no telling what Warwick might do with the information.

Did creatures feel the need to stick together against human law? Were witches creatures? Was Sabine?

He interrupted that line of thinking and attempted to divert Megan's attention from where Sabine had been and any potential mention of their plan. "I was driving through the bayou—"

Megan held up a hand. "Don't help her." She glared at Sabine. "Fess up. What were you up to?"

The crow, Sabine's reluctant familiar, strutted up and down the center of the table, *creaking* and *muttering*. Sabine followed its discourse with narrowed eyes. Jean-Luc thought he might have to intervene to keep her from throttling the bird, but it was not as if either he or Megan could understand it. Not really.

"Tattletale," Sabine groused, then gave a severely truncated version of the past few days. "The Voodoo priestesses of New Orleans graciously got together and decided to find me a tutor."

"Who?" Megan asked suspiciously, a reasonable question since the felon Georgette had been her last teacher.

"The Bayou Hag."

"Hmmm." Meg poured herself some coffee. "Did you learn anything?"

"How to cut away the darkness at its root," Sabine said smugly. She hadn't shared that lesson with him.

"How?" He and Megan asked in unison.

Sabine retrieved her satchel from the counter and dug through it. The smug smile slipped as her search grew more frantic. "That Witch! She took it."

"What? Did you steal something of hers?" Meg asked.

Sabine scowled at her. "And what have you been up to while I was busy training? I mean, other than assisting in a jailbreak."

Megan gave Jean-Luc a betrayed glance before answering. "I opened her shop because some little witch threatened to start charging me rent, and I needed the money. I'm not going to help Georgette do anything. She's a criminal."

"So, just a shopkeeper? No trysts with the fae?"

"Yeah," Megan snapped. "I had a tryst with a wounded satyr who came to the door needing help. Heaven forbid I should nurse a wounded animal back to health. I know I'm supposed to reserve my nursemaid duties for mangy foxes."

Jean-Luc groaned, remembering how he'd failed to help when Megan called. The young woman poured corn into a porcelain teacup and set it in front of the crow, studiously not looking his way. Raking a hand across his face, he let out a breath. "What became of the poor beast?"

"What, my *delusion*?"

He winced.

"Well, first Carmichael came looking for Sabine."

"What for?" Sabine demanded before Jean-Luc had the chance.

"The usual, I assume."

"When?" Sabine asked.

"While you were out prowling the bayou and stealing from old women."

"She was young," Sabine said. "Sometimes."

Meg turned back to Jean-Luc and continued with her story. "Then this older woman who lives nearby comes in to buy something for her niece, but she wasn't actually there for her niece. I don't actually know if she has a niece, but anyway,

Carmichael gets testy and leaves, and this woman goes upstairs and takes charge. Then this older Creole man, Ol' Ben, comes and the two of them take the satyr away."

"Ol' Ben?" The name rang a bell, but Jean-Luc couldn't recall why, certainly nothing to explain why this man would suddenly show up out of the blue and cart off a wounded satyr.

Bertrand *creaked*.

"What was wrong with the satyr?" Sabine asked.

"At first, it—he had this oily, sooty stuff all over. He stayed mostly unconscious and feverish, but I didn't see any wounds. I assumed he came from the market, through that dark heart Warwick described."

Jean-Luc huffed, time to come clean. "I should have helped. I behaved badly, and I'm sorry." Meg and Sabine shared a wary look. Did they doubt he could help? The darkness threatened to rise, and he tamped it down so he could finish. "I've seen creatures from the other side at the French Market. This one must have broken free. I didn't want to believe it was real at the time. Then you called, and it—"

"He," Megan corrected.

"*He* was lying there, and I couldn't deny it."

"But you did."

"Yeah, I did." He huffed out a breath, and his vision remained clear. "It's not just the creatures. The human vendors on our side are becoming . . ." He searched for the right word. "Corrupted."

"Yeah," Megan's shoulders sagged. "Georgette mentioned that."

"What did she say after I left?" Jean-Luc asked.

"You know how cryptic she is. She wants me to bring her some enchanted trinket from the shop to help her get out." Meg paused and seemed to recalculate her words. "Yeah, so I said, uhm, I didn't have time to look through her jewelry. I was too busy worrying about the market. And she goes, *'Oui, they are pourrissent.'* Like 'putrid', but not. I guess that means she thinks they're corrupt, right? I'm never sure what she means when she goes all Haitian French on me. So, I tried to tell her about the satyr, but the call got cut off."

Sabine leaned forward, eyes wide. "What trinket did she want?"

Meg groaned and threw up her hands in exasperation. "It doesn't matter. I'm not bringing contraband into the jail to help Georgette escape."

Jean-Luc and Sabine's eyes met. Megan looked back and forth between them. She was perceptive enough by this point to know he and Sabine were up to something, but not what. It didn't matter as long as they could convince her to find the object and talk to the witch.

"Let's think about this." Jean-Luc rinsed out his cup and put it on the dish rack he'd bought before the women moved in. "Things are getting pretty bad, and she seems to know something about it. If she can tell us anything that would help, you need to talk to her. Georgette had an ongoing relationship with Baylur before he went after you. Take this trinket of hers in, show it to her, and tell her you need information first. Then leave. You don't have to actually give it to her."

"Lie to a witch?" Meg sounded wary.

Sabine shifted on the counter, and Meg caught the movement. Jean-Luc put on his good-cop face, rusty from disuse.

"You'll be in a room with a glass partition between you. No way to pass it off. Tell her you'll get it to her lawyer, then she can coerce them into giving it to her."

Megan's eyes darted around the room, not meeting his or Sabine's. She seemed nervous at the thought of confronting the witch. "Will they let me in? I mean, they say she's high risk. I'm assuming that's a risk to me, right?"

"I have a friend," Jean-Luc nodded, seeing the plan come together. "Officer Wilhelm. I've already asked him to arrange for a visitation. He'll get you in."

"When did you arrange this?" Megan eyed him suspiciously, then Sabine, who tried to look innocent. It clearly didn't come naturally to the petite thief.

"After I left you at the shop."

"Why did you do that?"

"Before I handed you the phone, Georgette told me she wanted to see you. She didn't mention your bringing anything. I hoped a meeting would—" He broke off. How could he explain that helping Georgette escape would make it easier for him to dispose of the witch? This object she wanted added a new twist to the plan, but Sabine was clever enough to improvise.

Jean-Luc shrugged. "Hoped that she might give you information to help me find the fae, and bring him to justice."

Megan studied him through slitted eyes, obviously not buying his excuse. She was no longer the naïve young woman he'd met last fall. He didn't know what she'd been through at the hands of that fae, but Jean-Luc would make sure it didn't happen again. He continued before she could think it through.

"You and Sabine go check out the shop, and I'll check to be sure Wilhelm got prior approval for your visit."

"Sounds good." Sabine hopped off the counter, dumped her coffee in the sink, and left the cup on the counter.

Megan rinsed hers, then Sabine's. "Uh, small revision to the plan, I go to the Sassy Witch alone. Georgette said not to let you in."

Sabine's head whipped around as if she'd been slapped. "Oh, but I'm going in."

Jean-Luc decided it was best to stay out of it.

Megan winced, probably anticipating a fight. "But she thinks you'll steal something."

"Oh, I will." Sabine slung her satchel over her shoulder and headed for the door.

Chapter 25

SABINE

Meg parked near the front of the Sassy Witch shop. "You'd better wait for me at the front door. I think the wards might have been designed with you in mind."

"Touchy witch." Sabine climbed out of Meg's oxidized red Buick. "I'll see what they're made of. Maybe I can snatch them to use for myself."

"Leave them alone. We're not here to steal. Not even wards. The shop is under my care, and I take that seriously. Now, stay put."

Meg went around to the back of the Sassy Witch to unlock the door, and Sabine followed at a respectful distance, right under her elbow.

"I told you to stay. You'd think being part canine, you'd be better at taking orders." Meg jiggled the key to get the lock unstuck.

"A fox is not a canine."

"Yes, it is."

"Is it? I guess I can see that." Sabine pushed Meg aside and crouched before the door with her lock picks.

Meg glared at her, which Sabine ignored. The lock popped with a click, and the door swung open. "I don't know why you locked it when it's already warded."

"It makes me feel better with the shop under my supervision." Meg stepped around her and into the shop while Sabine tested the air, then gingerly stepped through.

Nothing happened. The door let her in without hesitation. No zaps. No alarms. No explosions. Meg rolled her eyes, and Sabine grinned.

Now that Sabine had her alone, she had a few questions she wanted answered.

"So, the market. You stayed clear while I was gone, right? No fae-watching?" Sabine chided as she climbed the stairs ahead of Meg. She probably shouldn't harp on it, but Meg's attachment to Baylur had never made sense to Sabine. Noticing that the taller woman hadn't answered, Sabine came to an abrupt stop and swung around, coming nose-to-nose with Meg.

"Oh My God! You *did* go looking for him?"

Meg pushed her out of the way and went into the bedroom. "I still have questions."

"I can't believe you'd risk it. Haven't you had enough abuse at his hands?"

"If it's so unbelievable, then why'd you ask?"

"Pitiful."

Meg whirled around to face her. "You know what's pitiful. What's pitiful is your having to be literally kidnapped because you're too childish to admit you need help learning magic, then learning nothing while you're literally trapped on an island doing nothing else but being taught magic."

"Lots of 'literals' for one sentence, don't you think?" Sabine asked, rifling through Georgette's chest-of-drawers.

"You could've at least tried."

"Who says I didn't?"

"I say you didn't, because, so far as I've seen, you've been able to do everything you've actually tried to do. Ergo, you didn't try."

"'Ergo' what a—"

"Shut up. And get out of those drawers. It's not in there." Meg got on her knees and pulled out the two enameled boxes and put them on top of the bed.

Sabine joined her and immediately dumped both on the velvet bedspread and started digging through the contents. "None of this feels like it contains a breaking-out-of- jail spell."

Meg gave her a look as she pulled a gold chain adorned with emerald medallions from Sabine's pocket. "If it's not useful. Put it back."

"I didn't say it wasn't useful for anything. Just not for spell casting." Sabine examined a brooch and several rings, discarding each by throwing it over her shoulder, before attempting to put something else in her pocket.

Meg caught her hand and shook it until she dropped a diamond bracelet. As it tumbled halfway into one of the enamel boxes, Sabine spotted an engraved silver compact wedged into the lid. She dug her nails under and pried it out. It popped free, revealing a mirror on the opposite side.

Meg snatched it up. "That's it. Let's go. And keep your hands in your pockets."

Sabine dutifully shoved her hands into her jumper pockets with both fists full of jewelry.

"Empty hands and empty pockets. I said no stealing."

Sabine snorted. "Just a few mementos of my joyful time with the witch."

Meg cocked her head, hands on her hips, and waited for Sabine to turn her pockets inside out, emptying all the loot back onto the bed. "All right. Let's go before you get your sticky little fingers on anything else."

"Except that," Sabine pointed to the silver compact in Meg's hand.

Meg curled her fingers around it. "Maybe I should hold on to it for now."

"I've been thinking."

"Lord help us all."

"Funny," Sabine said, holding out her hand. "You don't actually have to show Georgette the compact, right? You could just describe it to her. If you come in holding it, what's to say she won't ensorcell you and get you to give it to her?"

"Thibodeaux said there'd be glass between us. She can't grab it through the glass."

"You sure?"

That seemed to startle Meg. Good. Sabine wanted the compact in her hands to be sure Meg didn't chicken out and actually give it to the lawyer. She needed to make sure it got to the witch.

"It's just, I already feel guilty about teasing her into thinking she gets it just so she'll give us information. I'm not good at lying."

"You'll learn. You just need practice. Now give it to me." Sabine grabbed for it, but Meg held it over her head, out of Sabine's reach, which wasn't very hard. "She snatched hearts from people's bodies, remember?"

"Just the one. The other exploded," Meg said lamely.

Sabine could tell her housemate was hedging. She doesn't believe me, Sabine thought, which pissed Sabine off, even though Sabine was definitely lying.

Meg gnawed on her lower lip, her resolve crumbling. "I'll give it to you before I go in, okay?"

"Okay."

Meg pocketed it on their way down the stairs. Sabine stumbled on the last step, and Meg caught her before she hit the floor.

"Be careful." Meg opened the door and waited on the other side for Sabine to come through so she could lock it.

"Always am," Sabine responded with a skip in her step, as she sauntered through the opening, and the door lit up like a Roman candle.

Chapter 26

<hr>

MEGAN

It serves you right," Meg said as they pulled into the parking lot behind the Orleans Parish Prison. "I don't even see how you could've taken the compact out of my pocket that fast."

The back door to the Sassy Witch had attacked Sabine on the way out. Apparently, it didn't mind thieves passing through as long as they weren't carrying Georgette's stolen goods in their satchels at the time. The tips of Sabine's hair were singed to a pale yellow. The brittle ends cracked and dusted her shoulders like jaundiced dandruff when she leaned back against the seat. She ran her hand through it, and it rained down.

"Could you stop that? My car's going to smell like burnt hair." Meg parked in the designated visitors' parking and cracked her window to air out the car. "You stay here. Seeing you would only start a witch fight."

Slouching down in the seat, Sabine folded her arms and closed her eyes. Meg slammed the door. Leaving the compact with Sabine was not ideal, but she'd been right about not taking it anywhere near Georgette. For all they knew, the witch could use enchanted objects to convince Meg into orchestrating a huge jailbreak. And the only one who would end up in trouble would be Megan herself.

Thibodeaux had assured her that she couldn't get into any trouble just talking to the witch. She just had to convince Georgette that she'd found the compact and would arrange to get it to her. Thibodeaux said he would take care of the fallout when the witch found out Meg had lied.

Deception wasn't really her strong suit. Thibodeaux seemed to understand. Sabine just mocked her 'lack of imagination'. Well, Meg would make a terrible thief, but they were about to see how good a liar she could be.

"You're not a liar if you don't actually say you're going to give it to her," Meg tried to convince herself, but she didn't believe her own lie.

Officer Wilhelm met her at the security check and introduced her to a younger officer, who led her through an obstacle course of metal detectors and locked doors. Her nerves ratcheted up another notch as the officer showed her into a room with a row of glass dividers. Luckily, the space was mostly empty but for one other visitor at the far end. The man shifted so his back was to her as he waited for his prisoner to be shown in.

The officer pointed to a hard metal chair, and Meg sat, facing a pane of glass smeared with fingerprints. The room was freezing. The guy at the far end leaned forward. She assumed his prisoner had arrived, but the partitions between each chair kept her from seeing them. She sat on her hands to keep them warm and to keep from fidgeting as she waited.

Supposedly, Georgette had been informed about her coming. So either the witch had decided to make her wait, or it was a really long walk from her cell to the visitation room. When Meg finally gave up and stood to go, the glass partition started to buzz. It rattled in its frame, and the door on the other side opened. Georgette strutted through wearing an orange jumpsuit.

How could she possibly look that good in orange? Probably magic.

Georgette's raven-black hair looked like it hadn't been combed since the night she was taken in from the Mardi Gras float. Dark circles under her dark eyes looked like bruises against her pale skin. Of course, the French witch could pull off the heroin-chic look. Meg resented her just for that.

Stay focused.

Taking her time getting settled, Georgette adjusted her collar, patted her hair, and winked at the officer as she left. Finally, she looked at Meg with a smirk. It was so similar to Sabine's. Maybe witchcraft just did that to your face.

Meg pointed at the handset and picked up her side. Georgette waved a dismissive hand and spoke. Her voice carried through the glass.

Thank God Meg had left the compact in the car.

Georgette leaned back in her chair. "Have you taken care of *ma boutique?*"

Meg fumbled to hang up the handset and cleared her voice. "Yes. You being a celebrated witch-felon has done wonders for business. I'll need to reorder soon. We're nearly out of everything. I can send order forms with your lawyer for you to sign."

Flipping her hand in the air, Georgette conveyed her complete disinterest in forms. "Just signed my name. The petite thief can teach you how to forge a signature, I'm sure."

"Forgery is illegal, Georgette."

"Not if no one knows."

"Yes, it is. It's still illegal even if nobody knows." Was Meg the only one left with any ethics? "I tell you what. If you have your lawyer draw up something like a power of attorney, then I'll sign for you. Otherwise, I'll have to re-close the shop."

Georgette leaned forward in her chair and looked as if her stare might bore holes in the glass. Meg leaned back instinctively. "You will not close the Sassy Witch."

Then, just as suddenly as Georgette's anger had flared, it dissipated. She stretched like a cat and gave a suspiciously sweet smile. "If you have brought *le miroir*, then you do not need to worry anymore. Mlle. Georgette will put all to rights."

"I told you on the phone I'm not allowed to bring you contraband. I'll meet with your lawyer and see what he can do. But first I'd like you to do something for me."

The witch's dark eyes narrowed. She leaned forward, folding her arms on the table between them. Her metallic nails tapped out a rhythm. Chill bumps broke out on Meg's arms that had nothing to do with the temperature and everything to do with those nails.

"What is it you would have Mlle. Georgette do for you?"

Why was it so pompous to always refer to yourself in the third person? Meg tried to distract herself with the question, but it didn't help. She feared Georgette's metallic claws could shatter the glass and rip out her throat.

Meg swallowed hard. "I can't believe they let you keep those nails in prison?"

An evil smile spread across the witch's face. She held her hands out in front of her, flashing her nails for Meg's approval.

"What nails?" she asked.

"Oh."

Meg realized no one else could see the two-inch-long pewter nails tipping the witch's fingers like talons. Meg only saw them because Georgette wanted her to see them. She wondered if the witch still wore her corset under that orange jumpsuit to cover the gaping wound in her chest.

Trying to shut out the image conjured in her memory, Meg persevered. "Something bad is going on at the French Market. You said it was decaying or putrefying or something. Well, it's getting worse. Monsters are bubbling up and trying to break through from the In Between. What do you know about it?"

Georgette leaned back, looking bored. "What concern are monsters to Mlle. Georgette? I am in here. They are out there. If you give me *le miroir*, then maybe I become concerned."

"No, it's getting dangerous out here for the rest of us." Meg surprised herself at the animosity in her voice. "I want to know if you know it's going on."

The pewter talons scraped against the glass, leaving grooves behind. "I could rip your face off and use it instead of *le miroir*, perhaps."

A muscle next to Meg's eye twitched as if she could feel those talons sliding under the skin, rending it from her skull. Her mouth went dry, and sweat slid down her scalp. She cleared her throat.

"It's in the car. Embellished with tiny roses and inscribed with curlicues. They can't see me pass it to you, or they will take it. Just sit here and talk with me until our time is up, so they won't suspect that I came here for anything else. Then I'll go to the car and . . . And . . ." Meg crossed her fingers in her lap out of Georgette's line of vision. "There's a cop who can pass it to you."

"Why should I trust you?"

"Because I am not Sabine."

Tapping a pewter nail on her pursed lips, Georgette considered this.

"True," she said and relaxed back against her chair with a sharp smile. "Procéder aux jambes des échasses. "

"Uhm, okay." Meg wasn't sure what jambalaya had to do with anything. Doesn't matter. Keep your story straight, she coached herself, nervously fingering the charms on her bracelet. A fingertip landed on the heart charm, and an image flared in her mind's eye of a rotting heart in Georgette's outstretched hand.

Meg flinched, tried to speak, squeaked, and tried again. "The Sassy Witch is doing really well."

"So you said."

"Uh, yes. The disruption at the market is sending tourists our way. Which is—" Meg searched Georgette's expression for the correct description. The witch's brow formed a sharp "V," her head cocked, waiting for Meg to guess. "Good. Yes, good. It is good. So, of course, we would like to *encourage* the trouble there."

Georgette's sharp smile told her she'd gotten that one right.

"Sooo," Meg tried to guess what to say next. How to get the information she needed without having her face ripped off. "If I knew what was going on over there, I could throw gasoline on the fire, so to speak."

"You say the Faerie Market, it bleeds through, oui?"

Meg nodded.

"The heart of it, it feeds on the vendors, and they gain sustenance from it. Its center has gravity, drawing those with *intent sombre*." The witch gave a wicked smile, chilling Meg's blood. "The tainted ones, they consolidate and draw *la magie noire* to them, and they feed on one another."

Meg swallowed twice before she could speak again. "If the police wanted to stop this feeding frenzy, how might they do it? You know, so I can prevent it."

Georgette threw her head back and laughed. "They will not. As long as they carry a Writ of Business, they stay, and they feed."

"And if they don't have these ritzes, writs, rips?"

"Without a Writ of Business, the market has no use for them. It gnashes them to pieces."

"Oh well, we want whole vendors and a well-fed market, don't we?"

"Absolument!" The pewter talons clicked together like knife blades.

Chapter 27

WARWICK

The evening's air hung heavy with humidity. Warwick could not remain cloistered in the wooden shed behind the witchling's house much longer. He needed the comfort of something with life running through it, preferably with deep roots. The two oaks trapped in the yard by a fence were young and inexperienced, but they were preferable to the dead wood of the shed. He rested his hand on a trunk and felt the vitality humming inside.

His despondency of ever seeing his home again abated for a breath. It did not last long. His attempt to gain access to the market from the opposite side had failed, thwarted by its minotaur guard. Warwick could not discover the cause of its decay from the outside.

A creak of the gate warned Warwick he was not alone. He stood with his back against the trunk, blending into the tree shadows. Bertrand soared through the opening in front of Detective Thibodeaux, who shut and latched the gate behind him. The detective rolled up his sleeves and sat in one of the iron lawn chairs, facing the gate. There he remained for hours as the sun gave up for the day and sagged low in the sky.

Warwick held his position and observed. As the sun silhouetted the chimney pots on the adjoining house, claws scraped on the wooden fence. A fox appeared over the top and perched there.

"Did you find a way in?" Thibodeaux asked.

The fox leapt down, sauntered over to the ceramic-topped table, and transformed into the witchling's human form. Sabine climbed into the chair opposite the detective and gave a sly smile.

"Of course I did?"

"Did what?" Megan Armand asked as she came through the gate. The crow greeted her in raucous delight.

"You're supposed to be my familiar, not hers," Sabine told it.

In its rusty voice, the crow replied, "*I am no one's familiar.*"

"Where did you go?" Megan asked Sabine, plopping down in the chair beside her.

Sabine spread her arms and gestured around her. "Home, obviously."

"You were supposed to wait for me in the car."

"I got bored."

Megan held out her hand. "Give me the compact."

Sabine cocked her head and smiled, that sly fox-like one. "I think I'll keep it for now in case I need to preen my whiskers."

Megan loomed over the seated witchling. "You don't even know how to use it."

"Oh, I think I've got the hang of using a mirror," Sabine said, slapping Megan's upturned hand.

Thibodeaux interrupted. "What did the witch have to say?"

Megan plopped back into her chair, let her head loll back, and let out a sigh. "It's Georgette. Who knows what she said, or what she meant? 'The market, it bleeds. And feeds. And tainted vendors bleed.' How do we stop them, Georgette? Pause for maniacal laughter. 'There is no stopping them. They have the ritz. That's all they need."

"Ritz?" Sabine asked.

Megan wobbled her head. "Ritz, writs, rips. Something like that, for their businesses. If they have it, they are untouchable. They draw together, and their power increases the gravity."

Ah! Warwick nodded in silence. Why had he not thought of this vulnerability? Megan had gained more information than she knew. In the shadow of the tree, he contemplated how this might work to his benefit as the tall one continued her rambling answer.

"I was thinking on the way home, if these bad vendors are drawn together, maybe we can disperse them. Relieve the pressure, maybe?"

Sabine drew her legs up into the chair. "Or, we could just take them out."

"We're not killing people," Megan said forcefully.

Not yet, Warwick thought. From the looks on Sabine and Thibodeaux's faces, they had the same notion. The trio of humans sat in silence for several minutes, ending when Thibodeaux snapped his fingers.

"A Writ of Business?" he asked, and Megan nodded. "That's a legal document under common law. If the Faerie Market demands you have one, and you don't, then you just stop doing business and leave?"

Meg leaned forward. "Yeah, that's what she said. Well, she said if they don't have one, the market has no use for them, and it gnashes them to pieces." She shuddered, as did Warwick. It was a gruesome deed to behold.

"If it's just a flimsy legal document, couldn't they just have it replaced?" Sabine asked.

"It is not so simple," Warwick found himself saying out loud.

"Warwick?" Alerted to his presence, Megan scanned the yard for him.

He had meant to stay out of the futile discussion, but he found himself drawn into this band of hapless humans much as vendors of dark magic were drawn to the heart of the market. And he felt the first spark of hope.

Thibodeaux squinted into the sinking sun. Sabine and the crow studied the shadows under the young oak tree. They would not be able to distinguish Warwick from the trunk unless he allowed it. Except each of them did eventually focus on him.

An unnerving development.

"*Cr-r-oak.*" Bertrand glided over to perch on a limb above the goblin. The detective stepped into the tree's shadows to make him out more clearly.

"You had one of these Writs of Business?" the detective asked.

"Of course."

Thibodeaux's brow furrowed as he calculated, and Warwick braced for the question. "Then why did the market spit you out?"

"Because I no longer possess one," Warwick said curtly.

"And yet the market did not chew you up?"

Warwick muttered in the language of his people.

Bertrand *squawked*, "*Tell them. Tell. Tell.*"

Sabine's eyes tracked their conversation until the goblin answered.

"Even though I no longer possess a Writ of Business, the market dared not grind my bones. I am of the Court of Philip I, King of the Goblins. So, it threw me into this wretched place instead."

"You could always leave," Sabine muttered from her place at the table.

He grunted in response.

Thibodeaux ran a hand over his face. "Enough sniping. Warwick, you no longer have one. So, explain to us how a writ can be revoked?"

"It would require an appeal to the Night Court, the ruling body of the Beyond, as you call it. But no one enters the Valley of Night without a summons." Warwick placed his hand upon the oak's trunk for stability.

"Is that what you were trying to do in the Beyond? Appealing to the court to get yours reinstated?" Megan came over to wrap an arm around his shoulders.

Much to his wonder, Warwick found it more comforting than the tree. Nevertheless, he stepped aside. "None who answer such a summons has returned in the last hundred years. And I was not offered one, in any case."

It was close enough to the truth.

"Forget courts and fairies," Sabine popped out of her seat. "Neither can be trusted. We don't have time, and we don't need them. I'm the best thief in New Orleans. I'll just go in and steal these writs right out from under their noses."

"Can a writ be stolen?" Thibodeaux asked.

Warwick's hands clenched, his knuckles cracking. "Mine was."

"So, it can be done."

None but Warwick could see the black tendrils snaking across the detective's irises in the dim light. The last rays of sunlight left the sky as they all contemplated their situation. Bertrand the Magnificent Crow broke the silence. He *tocked* and *muttered*, *creaked* and *rattled*.

Warwick gave a slight shake of his head, but the crow continued its litany of warnings. It accused each of them of harboring a hidden agenda and admonished them to open up. Sabine shot Warwick an accusatory glare, and he raised his eyebrows back at her.

"What did he say?" the detective asked.

"Doesn't matter," Sabine answered. "He's just grousing. We all know the obvious solution. I filch these scraps of paper from the vendors. You know I can do it with one paw tied behind my back."

Warwick looked down his considerable nose at her. "Writs of Business are rarely inked onto scraps of paper." He turned his attention to Thibodeaux. "Therefore, the thief will be caught and likely caged, probably with a fire drake or chimera."

The crow *squawked* in dismay.

Sabine waved a dismissive hand at the bird and headed for the back fence. Megan stepped into her path. "You can't just leave. We haven't decided on a plan."

Thibodeaux's eyes went black as night. "There's no way you're going to the market alone."

Ignoring him, Sabine dodged around the tall one, fell into fox form and leapt for the fence. Megan's long legs took her there in two long strides. She grabbed the fox by the hind leg and held on. The witchling reverted to her human form, straddling the fence, and glowered down at her housemate.

"Let go," she snarled. "This is not some heist movie. We're not all picking parts and coming up with an elaborate plan that is sure to fail. Not when we all know I'm the best equipped to do this."

Megan did not let go. "It sounds like you don't even know what it is you're going to be stealing."

"I'll figure it out."

Bertrand landed on the fence and plucked at the thief's hair, grooming her. If it was an effort to calm Sabine, Warwick doubted pecking at her head would be effective. But he was too busy deducing how he might benefit from the witchling's impetuousness to mention it.

Megan tugged at Sabine's leg until the witchling lost her seat on the fence and tumbled. The detective sprinted across the yard, catching her before she hit the ground. She morphed into fox form midair and nipped at his sleeve. He deposited her on the ground, where she shook herself indignantly, and transformed back.

Her transformations had grown smoother and more immediate than Warwick would have expected from one of such meager talent. He may have underestimated her.

Sabine brushed herself off. "I didn't need saving."

"You never think so, but you always do," Megan said.

It became painfully clear that another bickering session was brewing. How had he allowed himself to become part of this wretched farce? They would get themselves killed or worse? And did he care?

Damn it all. He did.

If it came to it, he would reconcile himself to their loss if it met his ends. For now, the witchling's half-formed plan would serve him. Putting the market to rights was a boon, as Prince Pierre had said. Yet Warwick needed a greater offering to ingratiate himself with the ruthless King Philip. Bringing his Writs of Business from the most powerful, the darkest, the most corrupt vendors operating at the Faerie Market would surely buy Warwick's way back into court.

"Megan Armand is correct. We need a plan." He gestured to the table. "Shall we sit and puzzle out our heist?"

Megan beamed.

Sabine Scowled.

Thibodeaux's eyes cleared.

Taking this as agreement, Warwick stood next to the table, unwilling to sit upon the iron chairs, but his stature put him at head height with the rest once they were seated.

"And Your Magnificence." He waved for Bertrand to join them. Once the crow landed in the middle of the sunflower tile-work, Warwick began.

"The market's guard will not allow me inside the market." *Which is why we will need to distract him,* Warwick thought. "The tall one has the unique ability to enter the In Between and leave at will. She is the logical choice to procure the writs." He knew Megan would hand them over to him. He doubted the same of the thief.

Megan ducked her head to hide a smile. The naïve young woman did not realize she would be in harm's way. But regrettably, it was necessary.

Sabine barked her disapproval. "The fae will be on her like white on rice as soon as she enters the In Between, and you know it."

Warwick grimaced. Trust the witchling to intuit his nefarious plan. Without a decent retort, he ignored the accusation.

Thibodeaux took up the thread. "I might be able to get inside, too. I can watch her back. I've made an ally, or a potential one at the Faerie Market."

"Who?" they all asked, and Bertrand's croak echoed the sentiment.

"The bullheaded guard."

"The minotaur?" Sabine's eyes went wide.

Thibodeaux nodded. "I offered my assistance, and he didn't gore me. So, I assume we have a tentative alliance."

These humans were quite resourceful.

Sabine was being her obstinate self. "And what are you going to do if Baylur does make a move on Meg? Put him in a headlock?"

"Use this." The detective pulled an enchanted pocket watch out. It held its owner captive in a miasma of darkness. This timepiece had trapped Thibodeaux at a murder scene last fall, where no one could see him. It would have taken his life if it had been attuned to him.

Sabine jabbed an accusatory finger. "You said you got rid of it."

"Yet you have kept it all this time." Warwick mused. The dark must have a stronger hold on the honorable detective than Warwick thought. "Very well. You can accompany Missus Armand inside."

"What about me?" Sabine yipped.

"*Cr-r-oak.*"

"Indeed." Warwick nodded at the crow and cut his eyes to Sabine. "Megan is less impulsive and less likely to cause additional misfortune than you."

"I am *not* impulsive." Sabine glared at the goblin and crow. "I might not have an enchanted bracelet or watch, but I have talents."

"She is an excellent thief," Megan offered to mollify her.

"And I'm a *witch*."

They all grunted, revealing their thoughts about her abilities with magic. Sabine's hands balled into fists. "You all saw me on the parade float. I was throwing spells left and right. I saved all your asses."

Warwick winced, fearing she might unleash a round of wild magic.

"Don't take it hard." Megan draped an arm over the smaller woman's shoulders. "You can come. Every heist needs a thief."

"This one does not. You and I can handle the market, Megan. Sabine can wait outside with Warwick."

"The hell I can."

Thibodeaux's eyes clouded again. Warwick felt the detective's overprotection of the witchling was unwarranted and potentially detrimental to the goblin's ultimate goal. He did not trust her. It would be best if the detective kept an eye on both women.

"You speak as if you could keep the little thief out," Warwick said. "Megan can distract. The thief can thieve, and you, detective, can protect."

"What about you?" Megan asked Warwick. "You know the market best. You know what we're looking for. That makes you the most indispensable part of this group."

Sabine groaned at the pandering, but the tension between her and the detective dissipated for the time being.

"I fear my main employ in this endeavor will be knowledge."

"*Creek Creek Creek.*"

Warwick gave a shallow bow to the crow. "Indeed, Bertrand. You have shown yourself to be a most capable messenger."

"Spy," Sabine said.

Warwick continued. "The Magnificent Crow can carry messages there and back. If the thief has trouble identifying the writs, she need only send a query to me for confirmation."

The bird bobbed its head and began preening its feathers.

Sabine huffed at the bird. "How am I supposed to locate the documents?"

Warwick steepled his fingers and took a deep breath. He needed those writs. They would earn him admittance once more into the Great Goblin Court, but could he trust the thief to bring them to him? No, he could not.

"Well?" she demanded.

Then, a beautiful plan blossomed. With the minotaur distracted by the trio of humans in the middle of his domain, he would not notice a spare goblin. Warwick need only keep the thief occupied on a fool's errand. That should not prove difficult.

"Hey, Goblin, here." Sabine snapped her fingers. "The writs, if they're not on paper, what do they look like?"

"It will not be pleasant, I fear." Warwick chuckled, covering it with a cough. "Each booth will have a unique document depending on its wares. It will blend in. A writ is spellbound to the most loathsome artifact in each vendor's collection. It causes revulsion in a buyer, thus they are turned away from handling it."

Sabine narrowed her eyes, but with so little knowledge of magic, she could not argue.

"What does Sabine do with the writs once we're out?" Megan asked.

Warwick conjured his most solemn expression. "I will take the burden of such evil artifacts and properly dispose of them."

"*Caw. Ca—*"

Warwick interrupted the crow's protests. "I will station myself close at hand, perhaps in the establishment we patroned once, Detective Thibodeaux. The Priory, I believe. Bring them to me when you exit." Stifling a smile, he laid out the configuration of the market for them.

"How will we know which vendors are corrupt and which are not?" Megan asked.

"Likely, they all are tainted at this point. So, best to take writs from each.

"But they will be gnashed."

Poor innocent Megan Armand, what did you think would happen? Warwick thought, but he hung his head and said, "They are beyond redemption."

Megan gave a heavy sigh. "Will it begin at once? Will we have to see it?"

This bit of comfort he could offer her. "No, the market will tally its debts at dawn, then they will be no more."

"Will the market rebuild?"

"We can hope," he said, unsure if he meant it.

A grunt gave Thibodeaux's thoughts on the matter. He stood. Once again, taking charge. "Right, tomorrow eve will be the quarter moon. We meet at The Priory at sunset."

Meg looked it up on the map function on her phone and verified the time of sunset. "Got it."

Sabine shrugged. "I'll find it."

"*Cr-r-reek.*" Bertrand summed up Warwick's wariness of the efficacy of succeeding with a plan involving so many humans.

"Warwick?" Thibodeaux searched for him to get confirmation that the goblin understood the plan, but Warwick had already disappeared into the shadows.

The goblin had to plan his next move.

Chapter 28

CARMICHAEL

A frantic blare tore Carmichael from a nightmare where gruesome creatures watched as a man in a red hat ripped a beast to pieces. Sweat soaked her shirt. The bleating continued as she tried to orient her consciousness from the horrific scene to her living room. She'd come home and passed out on the couch and fallen into fevered dreams where Baylur instructed his minions to come after her next.

Recognizing the sound as her ringtone, Carmichael reached for it and knocked the phone off the coffee table. She scrabbled on the floor for it and struck her head on the table. Finally getting a grip on it, she answered with a growl.

"I'm off duty. What is it?"

There was a pause on the other end of the line, and Officer Johnson spoke up. "You said to call if anything unusual happened with that witch, or that pickpocket, or the French Market."

His stammering irritated her further. "Well, which is it?"

"All three." He regained confidence, and his tone was cocky.

As glad as she was to be out of the nightmare and eager to get such news, Carmichael's gut roiled with nausea. She funneled her fear into anger. "Well, spit it out then."

"You're gonna want to come up to the Orleans Parish Prison. If it were me, I'd do it now, before shift change, but that's up to you."

Carmichael grabbed her blazer that she'd thrown over the chair next to the couch. Johnson agreed to meet her at the entrance to the prison to fill her in, saying it would be best not to discuss the particulars over the phone. Either he was an idiot or smart enough to be paranoid. Probably both.

Johnson lurked in the parking lot next to his car, like he was waiting on a drug deal. Carmichael whipped into the empty spot next to him, and he jumped back before she could run over his toes. She climbed out and headed for the door, Johnson filling her in on the way.

"The prisoner, claiming she's a witch, says she has info on Sabine Domingue. Says the pickpocket is wrapped up in what's going on at the French Market. She wouldn't give me details, but she slipped a note to the guard on night watch that I have keeping an eye on her. Says she'll only speak to you in person."

Once they were inside, Carmichael flashed her badge and headed straight for the high-security cells. Johnson followed. "Did you need me to take her to an interrogation room?"

"No, let's keep this off the record." Carmichael directed him to go back to his station. The guard on duty nodded at her as she passed through. This wasn't the first time Carmichael had checked on the witch during the night. Her expression soured, knowing the detective's activities were against protocol but unwilling to argue. Carmichael had had to bend a few rules and wield a few threats to keep the guards quiet.

The lights were out in the witch's cell. They kept Georgette separated in an individual unit. She peered through the window in the door to see the shadow of the prisoner sitting on the edge of the bed, waiting. She'd known Carmichael would come.

That smug attitude was almost enough to send the officer back home, leaving the self-proclaimed witch to squirm in her jail cell. Much as she would've liked that, Carmichael wanted dirt on the little sneak thief even more. She signaled for the guard to release the lock on Georgette's cell. It slid open. Carmichael stood over the slight woman, whose sharp smile showed even in the dim light.

"*Le bureau veut le voleur.*"

"Speak English. I don't have time for your Haitian French mumbo jumbo."

In a heavy French accent, the woman repeated, "The officer wants the thief."

The door shut behind her, and Carmichael flinched. She resisted the urge to turn around and bang on the door until they opened it. They knew not to shut her in here. She clenched her fists and willed herself to stay still as the witch rose from the bed.

"How badly do you want her?" Georgette asked in an intimate voice. She raised a hand that looked to be tipped with long fingernails, flashing silver in the late afternoon light from the window.

Carmichael tried to step back, but the cell was too small. She'd have to retreat to the window, putting the prisoner between her and the door, so she held her ground as Georgette caressed her cheek with the tip of her fingernail.

Carmichael flinched. "If you don't have information, don't bother calling for me again. I'll make sure you sit here and rot before you get your day in court."

The witch tutted. "*Tellement de rage.* It will age your pretty face, and I have use of it."

Carmichael slapped the hand away, slicing her palm on the sharpened nails.

Georgette brought up her opposite hand, holding a small circular mirror, which she flashed in Carmichael's eyes. There wasn't enough light in the cell to blind her, but it did. She blinked, hearing the cell door slide open and close again.

Sparks swam in her vision. When they cleared, Georgette was gone.

Carmichael beat on the closed-door, yelling for someone to open it. An officer came to the door. "Keep it down in there. Witch or no witch, I ain't putting up with your shit this morning."

"Get me the hell out of here," Carmichael demanded through the glass in the metal door. "The witch has escaped."

The officer shook her head and walked away.

Carmichael banged and yelled and banged some more. Pausing for a breath, she caught sight of the witch reflected in the glass. She looked behind her. The cell was empty. She turned back, and the witch's reflection stared at her.

What kind of trick had she played?

Carmichael's temper flared, and she yelled again, then shuddered as the witch's reflection mirrored her rage. Carmichael gaped. When the reflection gaped back, she screamed.

Chapter 29

WARWICK

In the dimming light, a mannequin stood against the brick wall of the building adjoining The Priory. It wore a silver satyr mask, a tank top with the words DON'T MAKE ME GO ALL VOODOO ON YOU printed across the front, and no bottoms. Warwick stood next to it, wondering if the people who made the mask had ever seen a satyr before. And if they did, did they realize it was real?

The humans' willingness to ignore anything from the Beyond served him well as he waited for the others. With their mechanical cars, they moved through the city at the pace of a giant tortoise. A lazy one. The pedestrians walked past without noticing him. All but one man with glazed eyes. This person stopped, leaned down until his nose nearly touched Warwick's, and grabbed hold of one of his ears and twisted.

"It feels like leather. But it's warm, like a living beast. You're not real, are you, little fellow?" He stood back up and cocked his head at the goblin. "Maybe I should go home and sleep it off." He ambled off down the sidewalk as Thibodeaux's car pulled up and parked across the street.

Megan Armand walked around the corner as the detective crossed to The Priory. Odd. Warwick would've expected the fox to make it here first. She could be annoying, but she was clever and fast. If he hadn't already known she was born a witch, he would have suspected she had some goblin blood. Her ability to move silently, along with her irritable nature, would've clinched it if she weren't so slight of build.

Hopefully, the contrary human would do as she was told this evening. If not, Warwick could work around her. It was his one chance to go home to the court of King Philip.

"I can feel the evil wafting off of it," Megan said, slouching against the wall next to him and wrapping her arms around herself.

Warwick wasn't sure if it was evil, but it was not good. He could feel it bearing down on him even at this distance. The pressure had built so that it felt like the barrier between this world and the In Between could burst at any moment. He wondered if it already had on the other side.

Thibodeaux stepped up onto the sidewalk and stood beside Megan, looking into the window behind the mannequin. A quick look showed Warwick the detective was watching the market's reflection in the glass. Thibodeaux, too, was clever, another strong goblin trait. However, he could not be of goblin stock. If he were, he would not still be fighting to save the people of this city. If that kind of dark magic had taken root in a goblin, he would have taken over the city by now. Warwick knew he would have.

Nevermind. He was leaving this realm soon.

The last of the human vendors had packed their metal cars and were pulling away from the market. The glaring lights went out, and a heartbeat later, the faelights ignited. It astounded Warwick that the humans could not see it.

"Where is Sabine?" the detective said, irritation scoring his voice. His fists clenched, and his shoulders were taut like a warrior spoiling for a fight. "We don't have time to waste."

Of course, the detective would be able to feel it. He was about to burst from the pressure of the dark magic inside him, as well.

"The fox will be here," Warwick said without doubt. Of all the irritating traits the little one possessed, her loyalty was strong. "If you would like to start, we can see if I am able to enter with Megan Armand at my side." He volunteered, knowing it would not be so. He could not enter until they distracted the minotaur, but he chose to let his companions make the case for him, thus throwing suspicion away from his alternate plan.

"We've already been over this, Warwick." Megan shifted, bumping into the mannequin and knocking its mask askew. She straightened it out. Read the T-shirt. Then said, "I don't want you going in and getting trapped. I don't like Thibodeaux going in either. But you know he's not going to stay out with Sabine in there. I don't even like me going in. But we'll do it like we planned. Heists always fall apart when people start going off script."

Who knew what the tall one was going on about? She had a tendency to say a lot of words without any meaning when she was nervous. Warwick found it interesting that he recognized this characteristic of hers. It disturbed him to realize he would even miss it when he was gone. He had stayed here too long.

"The market is about to burst wide open. We go in now and get this done. Or it will be too late." As he pushed away from the wall, Megan Armand caught his arm, and warmth went up from the spot straight to his chest. Warwick had not known how cold he was until her warm fingers wrapped around his arm. She started to protest again when a red fox shot around the corner, headed straight for the market. Bertrand followed tight on her tail.

"There she is," Thibodeaux said with a note of resignation. "Game on, folks." He started after her.

Megan crouched next to Warwick. "Stay safe. Will need you for the next phase. Okay?"

Warwick pulled his arm out of her grasp and stepped back behind his stolid companion, the manikin.

Megan's face scrunched in a look that he would have called concern. But there was no call for such an emotion. He waved her on, and she took off at a jog to catch up with the others.

Warwick waited for his temporary companions to disappear into the market before he made his move.

Chapter 30

MEGAN

Street lamps lit the sidewalk around the French Market. Each had a hazy glow from the humidity in the air, looking ethereal and unreal. At the end of the block, a very Georgette-esque woman sauntered toward the empty market. Meg sprinted across the street and bent to catch Sabine's hand, keeping her from diving into the market alone. Jerking the smaller woman to a stop, she pointed to the suspicious woman.

"Is that Georgette?"

In typical Sabine fashion, she paid no attention to Meg's question, and fussed at poor Bertrand instead.

"What're you doing?" Sabine snapped at the loyal crow, hopping along the sidewalk beside them. When Meg looked back, the witchy woman was gone. Oblivious, Sabine continued lecturing Bertrand. "Put that down and focus. We're not here for shiny objects."

Bertrand had stopped to peck at a bottle cap, then a penny. He picked it up in his beak and offered it to them. Meg took it and put it in her pocket. They could use the luck. He bobbed his head and pecked at a strand of beads, flipping it with his beak and accidentally looping it around his neck. Meg suspected he was just as nervous about entering the market as she was, and shiny objects comforted him.

Bertrand hopped to catch up with them, and his claws tangled in the beads. He *croaked* for help.

Sabine knelt down beside him. "Focus, Bertrand." She spoke with more gentleness than usual when addressing her familiar. He flapped and *creaked* as Sabine un-looped the strand of beads now twisted around his wing. She stood, stuffing the beads into her satchel.

"Keep your beady eyes alert. This is dangerous." Sabine made eye contact with Bertrand and then Meg. You treasure shiny objects as much as any crow, Meg thought.

Ahead, a huge man stepped out from underneath the pavilion. His shoulders were twice as big as any man she'd seen before. His head seemed oversized, and he wore an angry sneer, like a raging bull.

"I'm guessing that's your minotaur?"

Neither Sabine nor Thibodeaux answered. It was just as well. Meg tended to ask useless questions when she was nervous, and she knew it. The hulking man looked at Sabine and snorted. That was really answer enough. More than she needed, really.

Oh, my god! I'm rambling even in my own head.

Thibodeaux headed off the man to discuss their entrance. If the guard allowed it, the detective would accompany them in to protect her from Baylur. She knew she could trust him. Even with the black magic inside that Sabine worried about, Meg knew at heart he was still a defender of good.

Great, now I sound like a superhero movie damsel.

Sabine's hand tightened on Meg's, dragging her around the far side of the column to get away from Thibodeaux and the minotaur, then let go.

Meg realized her hands were sweaty and scrubbed them on her jeans. "Do we just walk in? I don't see it. Do you? I don't remember how it worked before. It's like it was just there."

"We just keep pushing towards the center till we get there. You can feel it, right?" Sabine asked. "It feels slimy." She didn't sound any more confident than Meg felt, but they trudged on as if walking against hurricane winds.

The pressure against her chest was so strong that Meg could barely take in air. Sabine fell back a step, and Meg wrapped an arm around her shoulders and pulled her along. Bent over, they fought against the Faerie Market's attempt to keep them out. Sucking in what might be her last breath, the pressure broke. Meg and Sabine stumbled into an eerie scene.

On her first day in New Orleans last fall with her old roommate Valdi, Meg had been enthralled by the otherworldly beauty of the Faerie Market. Golden light shone down from orbs floating in the air. Colors in spectrums she hadn't known existed adorned booths full of fairytale objects. The enchantment of it lingered with her.

This was not that market.

This market felt rotten. The glow of the lights dimmed before reaching the tables. The delicate, jeweled masks had been replaced by snarling faces carved into wood so dark it looked burnt. Eyes followed the two of them as they walked between the booths. Something brushed her leg, and clawed fingers wrapped around her ankle from the shadows under the tables. Meg pried them away and heard a sinister giggle.

"All right. Let's make this quick, okay? I'm not sure how long I can stand this without screaming." Meg looked around when she didn't get an answer, and Sabine was already gone.

She didn't see whether Thibodeaux had made it in amongst the densely packed booths or if he was still negotiating with the minotaur.

"*Cr-r-r-uck*." Meg found Bertrand perched on a post nearby.

"We've got this. I distract the vendor from Sabine while she does her thing. Thibodeaux'll be here. He'll have my back, and I've got the bracelet."

A creature leaned over his table, leering at her. "You would like to see a bracelet, you say?" Its skin was raw and peeling like pictures she'd seen of radiation burns.

Talk, she told herself silently. Sabine needed time to find the object holding his Writ of Business. How could these creatures hold to such legalese?

Stop asking yourself questions and start distracting the vendors.

"You, uh, sell jewelry?"

"See anything you like?" The creature waved its hand. Under the trinkets, the black table covering undulated. Her skin crawled when she realized that it wasn't a tablecloth, but a swarm of beetles rolling over and around one another. Some stopped to eat their fellow insects. Their bodies glistening in the dim light, reflecting inky shades of the deepest blues, greens, and burgundies.

Oh, that green was not from a shell but from the inside of a half-eaten beetle.

The vendor picked one up with its long insectile fingers and held it out as if it were a precious jewel. Meg considered asking if it was a pendant or a ring when the vendor whipped a needle out of thin air and pinned the beetle to her shirt. It wriggled and clawed at the fabric as yellow ichor dripped from the cracked shell down her breast.

Bertrand *creaked*.

"Lovely," Meg choked out. Warwick had warned her never to accept a gift from the market. Ironic, since the charm bracelet that had started her venture into the Beyond had been a gift from him. With the tips of her fingers, she unpinned the impromptu brooch and set it back on the table, where another beetle snatched it up in enormous mandibles. She hoped that counted as a return.

Bowing her way back from the table, she went to the next vendor in hopes that that was where Sabine was headed. Its heavy drapes drank in the dim light. Inside the enclosure, intricate wire cages hung from stout chains. Glass globes swung from webbing, giving off a twinkling light.

Meg's chest loosened. Not all the beauty was lost from the market. Not seeing the merchant, she stepped inside looking for Sabine. There was no sign of the fox. She accidentally walked into a globe, setting it bobbing over her head. A high-pitched shriek of anger came from the same direction. When the globe stopped moving, Meg got a closer look.

Inside, a creature that looked like a child with serrated teeth and lavender skin clawed at the bubbled glass. It alternately gnashed its teeth in rage and wailed as if in agony. She found herself reaching for it, unsure what she would do once she had it in her hand. Maybe break the glass to set the creature free? Maybe secret it away in her pocket to ask Warwick what to do about it?

"The lady has a delicate sensibility." A woman, or a woman-like creature, with multiple sets of breasts hanging from an emaciated chest, brushed against Meg's arm.

"I was just admiring the lively little critter. Do you set them free after the close of market? When you no longer need them for light," she asked.

The woman wrapped a bony arm around Meg's waist and hugged her to her side. "Once you've caught them, you can never let them go," she whispered into Meg's ear. "Or they will gnaw all the skin from your bones quicker than you could snap them in half."

Meg's entire body shuddered at the touch, at the voice, at the thought. "Best keep them closed up tight then." She gently extricated herself from the woman's hold.

"If you are interested in something more gentle, might I suggest an owl?" The woman gestured to a brass cage big enough to hold a puppy. Inside, perched a forlorn tawny owl. Meg resisted the urge to check the owl charm on her bracelet to see if it was the hobgoblin she had met in the Midnight Jazz Club last fall.

Its snowy face turned towards her. Its soulful eyes blinked. And before Meg realized what she was doing, she asked, "How much for it?"

Warwick didn't say she shouldn't buy anything.

Meg started pulling remnants from her pockets. Who knew what his creatures wanted? "A ticket stub to a movie no longer playing?" she offered. "No?"

The woman looked her up and down. "An eyeball. Just one."

Meg's eyes flew wide open, and the woman took a step closer.

"No!" she shouted. Patting herself down, she came up with, "A penny, two hair ties, and a bent paperclip?"

The owl ducked, chattering, its speech hopeful.

The woman shook her head. "What about your pinky finger at the second knuckle?"

Meg shook her head.

"To the first knuckle?"

The owl cocked its head at her and blinked an appeal.

Bertrand *shrieked* a warning from above, probably jealous. Poor thing.

Meg wiggled her fingers in front of her face. Her charm bracelet dangled from her wrist. The owl charm blinked at her. How often did she use her pinky anyway?

"Oh! Yes! The bracelet! I will take the bracelet with the charm!" The woman said, her eyes reflecting the light from the trapped creatures and the globes. "I will have it."

She reached for Meg's arm, but Meg jerked it back.

"I can't. Those are my memories. I need them." The last time she'd given them up, she almost hadn't found her way home again.

The owl turned its head back over its shoulder in resignation.

"Would you give up the memory of me?" A shadow fell over her, and she turned to look up into the face of Baylur, the ice-cold fae who wanted Meg to offer her heart to him. She had been the first to ever refuse him. And just as Warwick had guessed, he wasn't giving up.

A black streak dove at the fae. Bertrand raked at his tunic with his claws. Baylur brushed him aside, and Bertrand fell to the floor, stunned.

The fae placed his slender, cool fingers on her cheek and let them trail down her neck to her breast. There they paused, and he let his hand rest against her chest, feeling for her heartbeat.

Bertrand *squawked* and pecked at her shoe.

Meg took a step back. Without taking her eyes from the fae, she begged the crow, "Go find Thibodeaux."

Bertrand shrieked and launched into the air, leaving Meg to fend for herself as the icy fae advanced on her.

"Your memory belongs to me," he whispered. "I will keep it safe. I will keep it always."

The merchant's expression turned sly and greedy as she said, "For the owl, I must insist on the memory of your first love."

Baylur's smile turned feral as he leaned down to ask again, his cool breath fluttering against her cheek, "Would you give up the memory of me?"

Meg swallowed, her throat raw. Giving up her memory of the fae would doom her to making the same mistakes over and over again, but leaving the owl seemed too cruel. "It's a deal. The memory of my first love for the owl."

The merchant grinned, exposing rows of razor-sharp teeth. She ran a hand across Meg's forehead and down over her eyes, pulling a memory from her, not of Baylur but of Valdi. The memory tasted of sangrias and smelled of stale college dorm rooms. It sounded like shared stories in the dark of night. It burned like fire on its way out. The remaining embers died as the woman removed her hand.

Tears stung Meg's eyes, but she couldn't remember why.

The merchant gave Baylur a malicious smile. He looked at Meg in confusion. The woman looked between the two of them, alarmed as Meg reached to unhook the owl's cage from its chain. The merchant's bony fingers closed on Meg's hand.

"The fae was not your first?"

"He was not even my last," Meg said. Remembering what Warwick had taught her, she added, "A deal's a deal."

"The deal was for the owl. Leave the cage," the merchant said, sounding sullen despite the rows of sharp teeth in her mouth.

Meg didn't know how she was going to make it through the market carrying an owl, but she was not going to leave it. The vendor unlatched the cage, and the owl stepped onto Meg's outstretched arm. It clung tight, its claws piercing her shirt sleeve. Its large, soulful eyes turned away from her as it unfurled its wings and took to the structure above.

Her heart was still tender from the missing memory, and the sight of the owl flying away hurt more than it should have. All she had wanted to do was free it, and she had. She didn't need a pet. What would Bertrand think of that?

A growl behind her was her only warning before Baylur lunged.

Where was Thibodeaux?

Chapter 31

SABINE

Luckily, Bertrand's compulsion to collect shiny things drew Meg's attention away from Georgette. Sabine wasn't sure how she would have explained the witch's escape from prison. She and Thibodeaux hadn't shared that part of the plan with Meg or the goblin.

Thibodeaux had told Sabine where to look for an easy way inside the prison. Which door was poorly guarded, and whom to follow inside. In fox form, she'd sneaked the enchanted compact to Georgette's cell, and waited and watched as the witch stole Carmichael's face. Genius and bone-chilling. Sabine had to learn that kind of magic.

Then she followed Georgette to make sure she went straight to the market. Predictable as ever, the witch did.

Sabine had hoped to get inside without Meg. She didn't need her to distract the vendors. It was too dangerous, but her long-legged roommate caught up with her, then spotted Georgette. It was almost a disaster, but for Bertrand's nervous trash picking.

Once inside the In Between, the stench of the rotting market burned Sabine's nose. She considered transforming back into her human form. She could sneak just as well in either, but fox form made it easier to weave between the booths. Sabine didn't want to keep Meg or Thibodeaux in this wretched place any longer than she had to.

Logistically, the two of them could both leave once Thibodeaux took care of Baylur. But Meg insisted on playing her part in the heist by drawing attention away from Sabine. And Thibodeaux was a stubborn ass who wouldn't leave until both women were out of the market. Chauvinistic pig.

His overbearing protective nature gave her a warm pang in her chest, because apparently, she was an idiot too.

At the first booth, while Meg played with the bugs, Sabine searched under the tables for the nastiest petrified crustacean she could find. Warwick couldn't give a specific description of each artifact that held a Writ of Business, but there was a clear pattern. Look for an object like the ones sold by each vendor. Find the nastiest of them. And snatch it. Easy.

Warwick had looked awfully shifty when he described them to her, but she wrote it off as typical sour goblin face. Then he got all solemn when he said he would 'take the burden' of them upon himself. What a load of goblin crap? Sabine didn't buy it for a minute, but he would know best how to dispose of them.

An enormous bug, the size of her hand, scuttled out from under a box. Sabine shoved it aside with a paw. If it was moving, it didn't count, according to the goblin.

Another, slightly smaller beetle with horns on its head and pincers the length of her pinky finger lay feet up near the back of the booth. She flipped it over with her snout and jumped back. But it didn't move. It smelled of mildew and misery. According to the description, this artifact must hold the Writ of Business for this vendor.

Gently picking it up in her teeth, she nosed open the flap of her satchel, dropped it inside, and moved on to the next booth following Meg.

While Meg made moon eyes at all the poor, pitiful creatures, Sabine ran along the back wall, sticking her snout into boxes and crates and cages. Finding a ratty, possum-like creature with stripes along its back and a cracked tail, she had to shift into human form to stuff it into the satchel. Hopefully, the rest of the items would be smaller.

They all felt dead and lifeless. Weird for an item that was supposed to hold something so venomous as a Writ of Business for a vendor dealing in black magic. 'Writ of Business' was such a mundane title for such a toxic artifact.

On her way out, she spotted Meg swooning over a hobgoblin owl. Bertrand perched in the structure above, keeping an eye on her. Trusting the crow and Thibodeaux to keep Meg safe, Sabine took off at a trot. She could finish faster on her own.

Slipping from booth to booth, she rooted out the nastiest objects she could find. Some crumbling. Some petrified. One particularly ugly, rotted wooden mask. Her satchel was growing heavy. But none of the ill humors of the market that vibrated around her seemed to come from the objects in her satchel.

After half a dozen booths, her tail brushed against something on the ground that sent a jolt through her muscles. They seized, and she fell on her side, writhing. Luckily, the drape off the table hid her from view. When her muscles relaxed, she sniffed at the object, a flat stone disk a little smaller than her palm. It hummed with corrupted energy.

Surprised, she accidentally shifted into human form and hissed. "You little son-of-a-goblin."

The stone disk emanated the black energy of the market. Had Warwick sent her on a scavenger hunt for a list of garbage, to divert her attention from these stones? If these stones were the writs, why lie about it? Did he want the market to keep rotting until it burst open, spewing its filth into New Orleans? Surely not. The goblin had many noxious traits. She could make a long list of them. But maliciousness was one of them.

Sabine fell back into fox form to prowl the stalls. Each one had a similar stone. Between a booth so dark that she couldn't make out its contents and one that seemed to be on fire, Sabine's fox nose caught a whiff of goblin, a familiar one.

Warwick crept behind the vendors, collecting the small, round disks humming with dark magic. His brow was creased with concentration. His hands were nimble and sure. And his mouth wore a smug smile that made her blood boil. He finished his circuit of the market with Sabine on his tail and exited out the opposite side from The Priory.

You rancid dung beetle, what are you up to?

Whatever it was, she wasn't about to let him get away with it. She'd known he was acting shifty. Bertrand had tried to warn her the goblin was up to something. But he'd also told Warwick that she was up to something, too. So, they'd both chosen to ignore the crow's warning.

At least Sabine's alternate plan involved something noble—vengeance. She doubted Warwick's was nearly as virtuous.

What nefarious purpose could the goblin have for keeping the vendor's Writs of Business for himself and lying about it?

Maybe he just wants a writ to get him back into the market, she thought in a rare moment of sympathy. She quickly shook it off.

Sabine stepped through the enchantment and watched from the shadows as Warwick secured his sack of stone disks and looked around for any witnesses. Looking past Sabine, he hefted the sack and tossed it over the wall running between the market and the streetcar tracks. Unburdened, he walked around the end of the market, presumably headed back to The Priory to wait for their crew to reconvene.

"Two can play at this game, you gnarly warthog." Sabine leapt onto the top of the wall and down the far side. In human form, she untied the sack and examined the stones. Should she steal them? What would he do? Handling them gingerly, she stacked the stones in her pack, which was nearly full of junk. The possum-ish creature taking up the bulk of the space.

The disks sent jolts up her arm. Gritting her teeth, she finished with numb fingers. Would Warwick notice her satchel was full of stones once she gave him the crap he'd asked for?

"No, let him play out his hand."

Pulling the stones back out, she hissed as her muscles seized. Once it passed, she resumed unloading the disks until her fingers caught on Bertrand's string of plastic Mardi Gras beads, and a deviously clever plan fell into her lap, or around her neck.

"Let the thief thieve, I believe you said," Sabine told the absent goblin.

Working as quickly as she could, Sabine stole the enchantment from each stone, relocating each Writ of Business to a separate bead on the necklace. She finished with two beads to spare. Refilling the bag and tying it shut, she fell into fox form, returned to the market, and finished her circuit. Before leaving, she found a particularly foul-smelling rodent and stuffed it in with the rest of the junk.

Serve the goblin right if he catches fleas from it.

Satisfied with her repugnant stash, Sabine padded between the booths in search of the others. Bertrand circled overhead, *squawking*.

Sabine regained her human form and called up, "What is it?"

The crow plunged at her, pulling up at the last moment to land on her shoulder, where he began *tocking* wildly. "*He came for Meg, and you were gone. I went for Thibodeaux, but he was gone. I went for Warwick, but he was gone. No one. No one. No one,*" he shrieked on repeat.

"Baylur came, and Thibodeaux wasn't there?" Sabine's muscles tightened, worse than a jolt from the stone disks.

Bertrand fluttered his wings, striking her in the face. "*The fae was upon Megan, and nobody was where they were supposed to be.*"

"Where is she?"

The crow shrieked, unfurled his wings, and soared over the crowd, repeating, "*No One! No One! No One!*"

Sabine fell into fox form and followed.

Chapter 32

◆────────◆

THIBODEAUX

The minotaur and Jean-Luc were of a like mind. Few words passed between the two of them before they came to an agreement. The guard would allow them in, and together they would rid the market of its filth. Now, if Sabine would stick to her task of stealing and leave the fae and witch to him, this would work.

Jean-Luc and Sabine had agreed, without involving the softhearted Megan, that Sabine would sneak the compact into the prison to aid in Georgette's escape. If it worked, the witch should make straight for the market.

Looked like step one was a success. He'd spotted the witch entering the east end. Luckily, Megan had not seen her former employer and current felon.

Once he stepped across the barrier between New Orleans and the In Between, the darkness rushed to fill Jean-Luc's every muscle. With each passing day, it became more effortless to let it rise, to use it. Here, in the heart of the market, it raged within him, filling him with power.

Shadows escaped through his pores. He breathed them out and fogged the surrounding air with darkness. It shrouded him so that he could walk through the Faerie Market unseen, even by these uncanny creatures. What power did they have that he did not? He was no longer a simple human, with no more than a badge and a gun to protect his city.

Jean-Luc was the monster now.

He prowled through the booths. Hunting the witch was almost too easy. He headed her off at the far end before she came near Sabine or Megan. Stepping up behind Georgette, he unfurled the shadows from his fingertips, letting them wrap tenderly around her. By the time she noticed, he had her snared.

The look on her face was one of horror. She knew this place. He had trapped her in the shadows once before in order to convince her to confess to murder. But her clever lawyer and psychiatrist already had a foolproof plan to get her out.

Jean-Luc would not allow it.

"It's been a while, Mlle. Georgette." He bowed deeply to her. "If you remember, the last time you were here in the mists. There was a watch. The one used on the man whose heart you ripped out with those metal talons of yours." He spat the words at her.

Her eyes narrowed as she calculated her next move. "What do you want this time? More words of confession? I will write whatever pretty lies you would like. I will swear to having killed every poor boy you let die on the streets of New Orleans. You can empty your guilt at my feet, and I will claim it." She smirked as if she were in charge.

"I don't have a timepiece anymore," Jean-Luc said. Not one he would part with. The old cracked pocket watch still rested in his pocket, an artifact he could not let go of. "Your time will not run out. You will remain trapped. How long can a witch live in the dark? Longer than I could have, I bet. I barely made it a week.

I bet on your lasting longer. Especially if you have someone else in here with you to keep you company.

"Let's see if we can find your companion. Perhaps if one of you is hungry enough, you could eat out the other's heart."

Georgette's hand strayed to her chest before she realized it and snatched it away. He had heard of the gaping wound there, where someone's rotting heart lay. He considered ripping it out, but didn't. Instead, he let her rage and scrape at the confines of her new cell made of mist. The black fog parted between her fingers and swirled in eddies, which closed back around her as he went on the hunt for her accomplice.

From his vantage point inside the mist, he saw the market in excruciating detail. The curses on each object glowed, eager for his attention. Vile monsters turned their heads to track his movements, wary because they could not see who passed. The black magic within him gave the name of each creature and told him the nature of their wares.

The beating black heart of the market called to him, and he answered. The witch was dragged in his wake, cursing and screaming, but no one noticed her. Her magic was nothing compared to his.

A streak of auburn flashed down an aisle between two booths. Everything else was in shades of dingy gray.

Of course, Sabine would be the one bright spot in the market. He quickened his pace. He had promised to protect Megan Armand. It was his turn to follow through on the new deal he and Sabine had made. She would take care of the market, and Jean-Luc would take care of their revenge.

In the depths of a booth with bright globes of screeching pixies and metal cages holding mythical animals, Megan bartered with what must be a selkie for a barn owl. Poor softhearted Megan. She did not know how to harden her heart. If it weren't for Sabine guarding her all these months, he feared she would've lost it already.

Baylur, the wretched fae, slithered up to her.

Jean-Luc could feel a malicious smile spreading across his face. He should feel guilty for using Megan as bait. He'd assured Sabine that he would not take his eyes off her housemate until he had the fae trapped, but he'd spotted Georgette first. Now, the fae was on top of Megan.

A *shriek* came from beyond Jean-Luc's shroud. Bertrand? Thibodeaux was too fixated on his current prey to pay attention to it, and the crow soared away over the booths.

"Baylur!" Georgette screamed, and the fae turned to look. His ice-blue eyes passed over the two of them, and Georgette cried out in frustration.

A dark laugh built up from deep within Jean-Luc's gut, where the black magic had first taken root. It boiled up and rolled out. The witch's distress was like an elixir to him.

Baylur reached for Megan's chest.

Should Jean-Luc stop the fae now, or once it had a dripping heart in its hand, catching the bastard red-handed? A laugh burned like acid in Jean-Luc's throat. Seeing the look of triumph followed by one of defeat would be glorious.

Then Megan Armand screamed, "Thibodeaux!"

Hearing his name called out as a plea for help temporarily jolted the detective from the darkness consuming him. Jean-Luc stepped out of the mists, wrapped his blackened arm around the wretched fae's neck, and dragged him back inside.

Baylur was strong and wrested himself out of Jean-Luc's grasp, but the fae could not escape the darkness shrouding them. The creature merchant searched blindly for the missing fae. Not seeing him, she slunk back into the depths of her booth, perhaps fearing she would disappear into the heart of the market next.

Fear marred Megan's features. Her hands flew to her breast as if she could feel those icy hands clawing out her heart. Tears streamed down her cheeks. She dashed them away and began searching the rafters, probably looking for the thankless owl she'd saved.

She was too gentle. Too good to do the things that needed to be done in this dark place.

Leaving her behind, Jean-Luc held the witch and fae in his confining darkness as he hunted for the minotaur. The bullheaded guard stepped out of the far side of a booth. His hand was fisted into the jacket of a stout man with bulbous eyes and scraggly hair, capped by a rust-red hat.

Jean-Luc let the mists part. The minotaur gave the detective a grave nod. Growling, the market's guard shoved the redcap into the dark prison with the snarling fae and shrieking witch. Jean-Luc had made a plan with Sabine to trap them there in the mists and let them tear one another apart.

He had promised once it was done, he would leave the darkness behind. He would leave the market before it consumed its vendors. He would rejoin their motley crew.

He'd made a lot of promises back when he was more man than monster.

None of those promises made sense anymore.

Jean-Luc stood at the center of the market, spread his arms wide, and breathed in its black magic. Power surged through him.

Why would he ever let it go?

Chapter 33

WARWICK

The masked mannequin made for a decent companion. It did not natter on about nonsense. It kept its thoughts to itself. An additional bonus, it drew attention away from him. Although Warwick barely needed a glamour at all to disguise himself against the brick wall of The Priory as he waited for the quartet to return.

These humans, even as clever as they believed themselves to be, were so easy to fool. Bertrand followed the trio into the market. He was a noble beast, but far too attached to these simple creatures. Warwick knew the honorable Thibodeaux would guard the women, and Sabine's ego would not allow her to send a message by crow to ask for help. While they were gone, the goblin had not worried that Bertrand would need to come looking for him. His job as messenger was ceremonial, though the crow earnestly believed it to be real.

With them off on fools' errands and the minotaur distracted, Warwick had plunged into the market to take the actual Writs of Business. They would be a gift worthy of securing his place back at court. The sack awaited him near the humans' iron tracks, where creatures would be loath to go. He would retrieve them after meeting with the others to complete this farce.

As Warwick waited for their return, he mused over the crow and witchling's relationship. Why did Bertrand speak directly to the witch? Certainly he was not her familiar, but what? She spoke harshly to the magnificent crow, but it was evident to Warwick that the witchling had a soft spot for Bertrand, and he for her. Both could more easily show affection to Megan Armand than they could to each other. Perhaps their companionship stemmed from their mutual sorrow at the loss of the older Domingue witch, Sabine's aunt. The crow had once been her familiar, but she had been murdered shortly after Sabine had come to study at her knee.

What of the hesitancy between Sabine and Thibodeaux? The only explanation for that was stubbornness.

Luckily, Warwick had avoided the encumbrance of an emotional attachment to these simple people. Soon, he would be done with them. Although he found himself oddly concerned for their welfare inside the corrupted market. He had need of Megan's aid one last time to return to the Beyond. Surely that was the cause of his apprehension, and no more.

Toward midnight, the women and crow emerged from the market. Step one complete.

Bertrand landed on the iron railing on the balcony above the goblin. The crow *tocked* and muttered and creaked, but did not make himself understood by Warwick. Something had the crow greatly unnerved.

A teary-eyed Megan fell upon him, hugging Warwick as if they were siblings parted for ages. But Warwick's siblings were back at the Goblin Court, not here. Warwick dislodged himself from her and faced the witchling who eyed him through slitted lids. Something had definitely gone wrong inside the market.

A spark of guilt tried to ignite in his breast, but he tamped it down and asked, "You have them?"

This step was merely a subterfuge to keep the clever fox off the scent of his true intent.

Setting the satchel on the ground, the witchling turned her back to him and began fishing items out and tossing them over her shoulder. Megan juggled and passed them to him. When his arms grew full, Megan found a discarded shopping bag, shook the road grime from it, and held it out so that he might dump the foul artifacts inside.

When she was done, Sabine picked up her empty satchel, and he noticed she wore a beaded necklace. Each bead thrummed with dark energy. Of course, the thief could not resist stealing something for herself. Warwick only hoped the necklace was not cursed, because he would not be there to save her from it.

Luckily, the most dangerous items waited for him behind the market. If Warwick were to enter King Philip's court carrying these false Writs of Business, it would be the end of him. A slow, gruesome end without end.

"Where is Thibodeaux?" Sabine demanded. Megan closed her eyes against the news as if she expected what was to come. Didn't they all?

No human could hold that much darkness and survive it. If it had not killed him yet, it would. And until that time, Thibodeaux would not be able to let go of it. It is the nature of black magic to take hold and not let go. Warwick doubted the Thibodeaux would be able to leave the market in his condition.

So be it. The honorable detective would go down as he would've wished, saving the people and the city he cared about, and punishing those who deserved it. Although on reflection, Warwick was not sure that the man he had first met would have meted out revenge so easily.

"Maybe he's waiting for us back at the house," Megan said unconvincingly.

"Yeah. I'm sure he is," Sabine agreed. "Meet you back there after your little detour to dump the writs."

What was she up to? The witchling never agreed to anything that easily.

Do not dwell on it, Warwick counseled himself. You are almost home.

"Okay." Megan studied her housemate warily. "I won't be long. St. Louis Cemetery is not that far out of the way. After I get Warwick into the Beyond and he disposes of the artifacts. We'll head straight there. We can celebrate with mint chocolate chip ice cream."

A wave of nostalgia hit Warwick. He quickly brushed it off and headed down the sidewalk. "Come along, Megan. I will wait for you at the cemetery gate."

"You can go in my car, you know. It would be faster."

Slipping into the shadows, Warwick left her to her metal automobile, and Sabine to whatever the witchling was up to. He need only gather the writ stones he left by the railroad tracks. Megan would not beat him to the cemetery. The magic of their machines was not as efficient as his.

As Warwick passed the market with a weary gait, he heard Bertrand's *screeching* and saw him disappear into the market after Sabine. Of course, the impulsive witchling would try to save the doomed detective, thereby dooming herself along with him.

Had Warwick ever thought it would be otherwise?

It mattered not. He had one last meeting to keep with the gentle, naïve Megan Armand. His only sorrow was that she would be left in this city alone.

Chapter 34

THIBODEAUX

Jean-Luc could feel the pulse of the market's dark heart. It beat in him and through him.

Until this winter, he was a detective with the force of the New Orleans Police Department. His job was to protect the city and its citizens. But that power had not been enough. People had died. Yet, even that had been taken from him. But he had this.

Magic. It worked. It gave him the power he needed to protect.

Did it make him a monster? Maybe. But it took a monster to fight among monsters. He could see that now.

Jean-Luc prowled the center of the market, daring anyone or anything to move against him. He ruled this place. Its heartbeat was his heartbeat. Vendors shrank back from him, and black eddies of wild magic spun in his wake.

The rusty "*Craaw, Craaw*" of a crow caught his attention.

Reveling in the raw power, he'd nearly missed the flash of color as he passed a booth. The shadows across his vision had reduced the market to black and white, yet this patch of auburn shone through. A red fox sat on its haunches inside the confines of an intricate brass cage. Its eyes met his. They widened in horror.

Had it recognized him?

The magic thrumming through him attempted to blot the vision out, to turn the auburn to gray, but it resisted. He knew this fox, and the crow perched atop the cage, *creaking*.

Jean-Luc reached for the vendor, wrapping a hand around the scrawny selkie's throat. "What is this?"

The selkie scraped at his hand until he loosened his grip. "It is a witch. She pretends to be a shifter, but she cannot shift inside the cage. Would you like her? It will cost you—"

Her haggling ceased as Jean-Luc shoved her aside and approached the cage.

"Who are you?"

The fox curled against the back of the cage, bared its canines, and snarled.

The darkness welled up in him, and he growled in return. How dare it bare its teeth at him?

"*Caw! Caw! Caw!*" the crow *shrieked*. It battered him with its wings. It ripped at his hair with its claws and aimed its beak at his eyes. When he grabbed for it, it flew out of his reach, then struck again.

Jean-Luc gathered a shadow storm in his hand and drew back when the fox screamed in a raspy voice. The familiarity startled him into dropping the shadow. The crow returned to its perch on the cage where the fox clawed at the metal, barking, snarling, and screaming in an almost human voice.

He turned to the vendor, letting tendrils of black smoke wrap around her midriff, chest, and throat. Air whooshed from her as the tendrils tightened. She choked and coughed and cursed, but Jean-Luc did not let go. The bands tightened, cutting into her flesh, cutting off her air, and threatening to cut her into thirds and quarters.

Leaning in close, he growled. "Let the fox go."

The selkie jerked her head, yes, and flipped a wrist at the cage. The door sprang open, and the fox leapt free. It landed at his feet in the form of a human.

Sabine.

Her tousled hair had fallen from its tie and lay about her shoulders, framing that serious face with intense eyes, which glared up at him. Her colors were muted by the veil of darkness across his vision. The auburn hair was dulled, leaving only a hint of red, like an old photograph. But it was Sabine.

She had come back for him, and the market had trapped her.

"Thibodeaux," she barked. "Let go of the magic."

He shook his head. How could she not see? He could save her because of the magic. The darkness inside him was angry and bent on destruction, but it was the only weapon he had to fight and win.

She took a step closer. "Drop it." Her scowl deepened.

The darkness in him reached out for her. Jean-Luc held out a hand to keep her back so that he could explain. "You have magic, Sabine. You think you only stole it, but I've seen it. Even if you can't always find it, it's there. It comes to you when you need it. Now, I have it too. It is the only weapon that works against these creatures."

Sabine shook her head and stepped in again, pressing against his outstretched hand. He could feel the growl rumbling in her chest. "This is not how you fight, Thibodeaux. You fight smart. You fight with your heart. Leave the darkness to those of us born to it."

Confused, he let down his guard, and his hand fell. "No. There is no darkness in you."

She smirked. Of course, she did. "Then why does it call to me? Did I tell you that? That it had wanted me from the first time I stepped foot into the Faerie Market. It drew me to it. If I let my mind wander, my feet lead me here time and time again. Didn't you listen to Warwick?"

He shook his head. "He meant me, not you."

"No, Thibodeaux. You are the thief here. You stole the darkness. It is not yours. It is mine. And I will have it back." Sabine prowled ever closer.

Too late, he put his hand up to stop her. Sabine's heart beat against his palm as they stood toe-to-toe. The darkness flooded down his arm, racing towards her. His breath caught, and he wrestled the black magic back. He would not let it have her.

"Sabine, leave the market and let me finish this."

"No."

Holding her in place, Jean-Luc took a step back. "This friendship, relationship, us, whatever it's been . . . Thank you for that. But it is over. It's time for you to go."

Sabine dodged around his outstretched hand, but Jean-Luc caught her shoulders. She was scrappy, but he was stronger. The darkness surged down his arms, and he shoved her away just as it reached his fingertips. It tried to jump the distance between them, but he clenched his hands into fists and fought as hard as he could to hold it back until she escaped.

She took a step away from him, and Jean-Luc clasped his hands hard to keep from reaching for the tough, stubborn, brave woman. Sorrow swelled in his chest and clogged his throat. The two of them were over before they'd even begun, but he was about to unleash death and destruction on this place. He could only hold it back for so long, would only hold it back until she was out of his sight. Then he would destroy the market.

There had always been a river running between him and Sabine. But now it was a gulf that no bridge could span. He let out a breath, trying to say goodbye, but the words failed him.

Sabine took another step away from the market's center, and Jean-Luc's shoulders relaxed even as the darkness crawled up and out. He grappled with it. Fighting so that he could not see past the blackness in his eyes.

"Run!" he yelled, praying she listened, just this once.

She did not.

Sabine leapt straight at him. Grabbing hold of his shirt, she jerked him close and snarled. "I said, Drop it!"

Gritting his teeth, Jean-Luc held the darkness in as it raged to be released.

Sabine's flinty expression turned soft and pleading. "Jean-Luc, please. Let go."

I can't, he thought, but he couldn't speak without letting the darkness escape.

Sabine snaked an arm around his neck. Her hand caught in his hair, and she jerked his head down hard, putting them eye-to-eye.

Shoving the darkness down with all his effort, Jean-Luc begged, "Sabine—"

She took the opening and kissed him. He tried to pull back, but the petite woman was strong and scrappy and stubborn. He'd always known it. How ignorant of him to ever think he could stop her.

Despite his resolve to keep her away, despite the ache to protect her and hold the darkness down, Jean-Luc wrapped his arms around her and pulled Sabine in, crushing her against his chest. If this was to be their goodbye kiss, he would take it.

Sabine tasted of cinnamon and coffee. Her heart thudded against his chest. His beat against his ribcage, trying to escape and join hers. For the first time since the black mists had taken root inside him, Jean-Luc felt the tension in his chest ease. He drew in a breath, his lungs expanding fully for the first time in months. The tension in his shoulders loosened even as his arms tightened around her.

Then, all at once, Jean-Luc realized what she was doing.

Sabine was stealing the dark from him.

He shoved her back, and she wore a savage, victorious smile. "NO!" he roared.

Black tendrils stretched between them. Sabine curled her fingers around them and yanked. Once a thing was in her grasp, Sabine did not let go. But this time, he would make her.

Jean-Luc reached to take a fistful of darkness, but it turned to mist and slipped through his fingers.

"No, Sabine. Let go. It is not yours."

"It is now."

She jerked, dragging it out of him. The black tendrils set hooks, not wanting to let go of him. Sabine ripped and tore at it until his insides were raw. The magic raked its way out, leaving him hollow. The connection snapped free, and he fell back.

The minotaur was there and caught him.

Unable to grasp the darkness, Jean-Luc grabbed Sabine instead, but she fell into fox form and ran. A monstrous shadow trailed behind her.

"Get her," Jean-Luc ordered.

The market's guard grunted. "You catch that rabid beast yourself if you think you can."

Jean-Luc sprinted after her, but he could not keep up.

The white tip of her auburn tail was now black. She flicked it back and forth as she ran. Threads of dark magic spun from the blackened tip, latching onto anything and everything that contained a drop of black magic. Which no longer included Jean-Luc.

The threads searched for purchase and found it, dragging the magic out of each cursed gem or statue. Sneering masks screeched as the magic was torn from them, and they fell to the floor empty. Vendors screamed in agony and chased the fox.

Sabine flew through the market, weaving in and around booths until she crossed the barrier and fled into New Orleans, taking the market's dark magic with her.

Jean-Luc stumbled from the In Between. Sabine's kiss had freed him, but the horror remained. How could the cunning sneak thief, the calculating witch, the clever fox, outrun the darkness clinging to her tail?

Chapter 35

MEGAN

St. Louis No. 1 felt empty as Meg and Warwick passed between the mausoleums. Cemeteries were normally quiet, sure, but last time they came, this one was filled with jazz from The Musicians' Tomb. Maybe their souls were at rest, or maybe they were busy elsewhere.

As dawn approached, she escorted Warwick through the crypt to the Beyond, where the stone bridge and rocky landscape waited. Strangely, Meg no longer feared this place. Sabine, Thibodeaux, and Warwick thought she was naïve and gentle. She had been both once, but her time in the Beyond had changed her. She was not so innocent as to believe Jean-Luc could make it out of the market unscathed, or that Sabine would make it out at all.

The detective had been willing to give himself up to save the city.

Sabine had been willing to give herself up to save him.

And Warwick had risked his king's ire to return to the Beyond and dispose of the Writs of Business. The stone disks clattered in the bag as the goblin shifted from foot to foot.

"You may return, Megan Armand. I will go alone from here." Warwick bowed deeply to her as if she were royalty.

"See you back at the house when you're done?" she asked.

"Of course," he lied, averting his eyes. He sounded so sad and solemn.

Meg started to put a hand on his arm, to give it a goodbye squeeze, but remembered how much he hated physical contact. She'd always known it, but it had taken her a long time to break the habit. She let her hand drop back to her side.

"Goodbye, Warwick."

"Farewell, Megan Armand." His eyes darted up to hers, and they glistened. It must be a trick of the early morning light.

After he crossed the bridge and disappeared from sight, Meg held up her charm bracelet. Locating the owl, she pinched it between her pointer finger and thumb.

"*Whoot. Whoot.*" A tawny owl landed before her.

"You're the hobgoblin who helped us last fall, aren't you?"

The owl shimmered and lengthened into a young man with tawny skin and thick circular glasses perched on his beak-ish nose. "I am."

"Was it you I freed in the market?"

"It was." He tilted his head until his ear nearly touched a shoulder, and he blinked again with his owlish eyes. It was really quite adorable. "May I repay my debt to you?

Meg felt the pang of the lost memory but could no longer remember the shape of it. Well, she had a task to complete. Worrying over a lost memory would not bring it back. "You can find things?"

He nodded and blinked.

"Where is the Writ of Business stolen from the Honorable Warwick, once of the Great Goblin Court of King Philip I?"

The man stood still, but his head swiveled to look first over his left shoulder and then his right. He shook as if fluffing his feathers before speaking. "A fae by the name of Baylur stole it."

"Ahhh," Meg said, the sound coming out as a breath. If Baylur had taken it, then she knew where it was. "Thank you," she said, bowing in case that was the proper way to thank a fae and say goodbye. As she straightened, the man fluttered, and a tawny owl launched into the air.

Meg set out for the ice giants' palace.

Chapter 36

SABINE

Sabine swerved through the Faerie Market. Her paws scrabbled at the concrete, propelling her between booths. Demons and goblins, fae and beasts she could not name, trailed close in her wake as she escaped the In Between.

The sky blushed as the sun threatened to rise over New Orleans. Hitting the asphalt, she wove her way through its gridded streets. Creatures broke free of the market and followed. She had to keep them close until the last tether snapped or they would descend upon the people of the city, most of whom had no idea they even existed.

As she ran past clubs, shops, and restaurants, closed for the night, ghosts leached from century-old brick buildings. They slipped through iron grates at the base of stucco walls. They shot out clay chimney pots at the top of chipped slate roofs.

Rising in a blue miasma over the streets, they howled and coalesced before plunging down toward her. The force of the souls' movement buffeted against her sides, knocking her off her feet before they whisked away, leaving nothing but a chill behind. Without slowing, she dared a glance over her shoulder to see a swarm of New Orleans's ancestors plow into the creatures clinging to the black magic attached to her tail.

An unholy cacophony of growls, snarls, and screeches unleashed into the pre-dawn streets as the two forces collided.

Shutters were thrown open as the mortal inhabitants of New Orleans searched for the cause of the chaos. They had no idea what they risked inviting inside.

The souls of the deceased slowed the creature's pursuit, dragging at the magic that did not want to let go.

Sabine trudged ahead, her claws raking the asphalt. Her muscles ached from the strain. Her bones creaked, and her joints were close to popping, when the thick black tether holding her to the creatures broke. It snapped back, throwing her head over tail down the street. She curled in a ball and rolled to a shuddering stop against an old brick wall with a loose grate at the bottom.

A familiar abandoned brick townhouse rose three stories to the attic, where Sabine had once made a hidey hole. Just like a fox, when her life was in danger, she'd instinctively returned to her den.

Bertrand landed on the sidewalk and hopped over to her. He plucked at the Mardi Gras beads containing the corrupted Writs of Business dangling from her neck.

"I've got a plan for them. Sort of. But we need to lay low until I'm sure no one followed."

"*Friend or foe*?" Bertrand *croaked.*

"Exactly." Sabine wriggled through the cast iron grate, leaving the ancestors of New Orleans to chase away its intruders.

Chapter 37

CARMICHAEL

Wearing yesterday's stale clothes, Carmichael careened toward the French Market. The blue light on her dashboard did little to warn drivers. Her headlights in the early morning gloom did more. If it were any later, she'd be gridlocked. As it was, she still cursed the cars daring to cross her path.

She'd worn Georgette's face for nearly an hour before it faded into her own. Maybe that bitch was the witch she said she was. It had taken a shift change the next morning at the Orleans Parish Prison for Carmichael to convince someone to come let her out. The prison guards were confused, and she was humiliated. Someone would pay.

Reports overlapped on the police radio of people calling in about a disturbance near the French Market. That's where Carmichael would start. Her car screeched to a halt, with one front wheel up on the curb. As the motor ticked to a stop, she jumped out and sprinted for the market.

Empty racks lay overturned and twisted as if a hurricane had come through. Carmichael searched the shadows for a fox or witch when an ice-cold hand wrapped around her throat. She gasped and turned to face Baylur. His once beautiful face was twisted into a monstrous snarl.

"The witch. Where is she?"

"Georgette escaped." Carmichael gagged as his hand tightened, cutting off her air.

"The fox," he said through gritted teeth. Ice crusted her neck and shoulders, running down her arm and torso. He loosened his grip so that she could speak.

"Why do you want her so bad?"

"The clever fox has prevented me from possessing the heart of Megan Armand. It is mine, and she is in my way."

Carmichael was nauseated to discover she was jealous, even as his fingers threatened to cut off her air again. "I-I-I know someone who can help me get her. I just need to convince him she's trouble."

He lowered his hand and stepped back, eyes slitted. "Bring the witch to me, or I will take your heart instead."

Visions of her heart beating in his palm flashed through her mind. Desperate, she risked speaking. "If I'm going to help you, I need to keep my job." She swallowed, and the ice around her throat cracked. "I need Georgette."

With an icy laugh, he disappeared.

Carmichael screamed in frustration.

Startled, a shadow broke free of a column at the far end of the pavilion. Carmichael sprinted after it. The morning sunlight cut across the river and through the market, revealing an orange jumpsuit as the figure disappeared behind the shops.

Carmichael cackled. "Got you."

Chapter 38

THIBODEAUX

Jean-Luc knocked on the dark purple door he'd repainted last fall. Eggplant, the hardware store had said the color was eggplant. He knocked again.

"You survived." A gravely voice spoke from the porch swing.

"So it would seem." Jean-Luc said, peering in through the cottage's front windows.

"They are not home," Warwick told him from the shadows cast by the ferns hanging from the edge of the porch.

Jean-Luc sat on the front steps to wait. "Did you get the artifacts out of the city?"

The porch swing creaked back and forth, back and forth, before the goblin answered. "I did." Warwick kicked a bag out from under the swing. It clinked as if it were full of rocks. "But then I brought them back. I was one of the corrupted vendors. I cannot be trusted with Writs of Business."

Jean-Luc did not respond.

The creaking of the porch swing ceased, and Warwick confessed. "I wished to use them to buy my way back into court. It was a dishonorable goal. I do not deserve a place in the Great Goblin court. You must deal with the stones."

Jean-Luc studied the sack out of the corner of his eye, but made no move to take it. Neither spoke again as the sun climbed the sky, and neither woman came home. Jean-Luc checked his phone for updates about the market.

"Chaos," the news said, and all outlets agreed. Chaos broke out in the early hours before dawn, blocks from the French Market. All trouble was cleared up before police arrived on the scene. Both residents and police are baffled as to the cause of the disturbance.

A text pinged his phone as he scrolled the news reports. "Report to my office by noon," sent by the NOPD superintendent. She'd called and emailed, and Jean-Luc had ignored both. When he did not respond to her latest text, she followed up with, "To discuss reinstatement." He pocketed the phone and waited as noon came and went and the sun slid down the far side of the sky.

Cicadas quieted in the treetops, and crickets began screeching from a ditch, announcing twilight. A faded red Buick pulled up to the curb, and Megan Armand got out carrying a silk bag swinging from a silver cord.

As she approached the porch, Megan asked, "Sabine not home?"

"No," Jean-Luc said, making room for her to climb the steps.

She glanced over at the goblin on the swing as she unlocked the front door. "You want some ice cream?"

Neither Jean-Luc nor the goblin moved nor spoke.

"She'll come home," Megan said in a soothing tone. "Come in and help me wait. It's no good stress-eating alone." She went inside, leaving the door open. They followed and sat at the wooden table where they had argued and schemed how to cure the market. Now they waited as Megan served ice cream.

Jean-Luc turned his bowl in a circle then tipped it toward the goblin, who shook his head. Warwick stared equally hard at his without touching it. Jean-Luc sighed and broke the silence.

"I'm sorry, Megan. Baylur escaped in the," he searched for the word and borrowed it from the news reports. "Chaos."

Megan sat down with them and stared at her own bowl. "I wouldn't worry over Baylur, detective."

"Oh?" he said, hopeful.

"Apparently the king of the ice giants made a bet with him. You get a heart, or you give a heart." Megan looked up through her lashes at him, and a devilish smile spread across her face. "And I still have my heart. So, Baylur loses his. Poor fellow."

"You went to the ice giants' palace alone," Warwick said, his voice gruff with a concern that surprised Jean-Luc.

"I did. The king allowed Baylur to hide there. That's where he took me when . . . Well," her eyes darted to the canvas bag, "I have a gift for you, Warwick, from Baylur's stash." She reached over her shoulder and pulled the silk bag off the counter. It thudded onto the tabletop. As she picked at the knotted cord, the front door opened and slammed shut.

Megan's fingers froze on the knot. They all waited, listening. Their attention was so intent on the dark hallway that a sharp crack at the kitchen window startled them.

A black form struck the window over and over, as if trying to break the glass. Jean-Luc reached for a pistol that he no longer wore. Warwick eased out of his chair and stood to the left of the hallway where he could keep an eye on the window without being seen from the front room.

"Don't open the window for that pestilent plumage," Sabine called from the living room, and relief washed over them.

She appeared in the doorway. Dusty and scraped and utterly alive. "He's been lecturing me all day. He can go roost on that scarecrow he's so fond of."

Megan jumped up, and Sabine flinched, probably expecting a hug, but the tall woman went for the window instead, throwing it open. Jean-Luc forced himself to keep his seat. Warwick eased back into the chair as if he'd never left it. Sabine's shoulders slumped, disappointed or fatigued. Jean-Luc couldn't tell which.

Bertrand burst through the window, *croaking* and *tocking*, his voice hoarse as if from overuse. "*Nobody! Nobody was where they were supposed to be.*"

"Yeah, yeah. You said that before." Sabine peered into the freezer, cool and casual as if they hadn't just fought for their lives against forces they didn't understand. As if Jean-Luc hadn't turned into a monster in front of her. "Still only mint chocolate chip?"

"You don't like mint chocolate chip?" Jean-Luc asked.

"No, she never has," Warwick and Megan said in unison, and Bertrand *croaked* in agreement.

Sabine smiled almost apologetically at him. So, she did know that he'd bought it.

"But maybe it's an acquired taste." She hopped onto the counter. "I saw your bag on the front porch, Warwick. You decide to keep the artifacts?"

Warwick slumped over his bowl and stirred the melted ice cream in a circle. "I am unworthy of taking the writs to the king."

Sabine's head cocked, and her brow creased. "That's why you wanted them?"

"What should we do with them?" Meg asked, stirring her own ice cream.

"We could trash them. It's all junk," Sabine suggested casually.

"You cannot toss such evil in the trash." Warwick snapped, then his tone eased. "The bag does not contain the artifacts you collected, witchling. I did indeed toss those into the river. They did not carry the Writs of Business. I misled you." Warwick's head bowed in shame.

"Did you?" Sabine said brightly. "Hmph, who would have known?"

Warwick raised his head and studied her for a long moment before the corner of his mouth curled into a smirk. "You clever fox."

Sabine shrugged.

"What?" Meg asked.

Bertrand strutted and *creaked*.

"Where did you take them?" Warwick asked Sabine.

"Not your problem," Sabine answered. She tried a bite of mint chocolate chip and winced.

"No, it is not," the goblin said with obvious relief. "Megan, dear, you said you had something for me?"

Untying the cord, Megan reached into the silk bag and brought out an ice-blue scarf wrapped around a small bundle and laid it on the table in front of Warwick. He unwrapped it, revealing a smooth, round disk of stone.

"My Writ of Business." Warwick made the slightest of sounds. If Jean-Luc had not known better, he would have suspected it was a sniffle. In a gruff voice, he said, "But I had not planned to return to this place."

"I know." Megan's eyes glistened. "But I'd hoped."

Warwick turned his head from the table, rose, tucked the gift into his coat pocket, and left without touching his ice cream.

"I'm grateful you both made it home safely," Jean-Luc said, standing to leave. "With Baylur taken care of—"

"How?"

"I'll explain," Meg said, and Jean-Luc continued.

"And Georgette's back in prison, according to the news reports. Things should be quiet for a while."

Sabine grunted. "Prison's too good for her."

"Don't worry about Georgette. She'll get what's coming to her." Megan retied the silk bag.

"How do you figure?" Sabine asked.

"I brought a present for her, too." Meg laid her hand over a sizable lump in the bag. Jean-Luc might have been imagining it, but he thought he heard a muffled thumping against the table. He chose not to ask any questions.

Instead, he tipped his chin to them. "I better be going. Early day at the precinct tomorrow."

"They're giving your badge back?" The hope in Sabine's eyes left a hairline crack in his heart.

"No, I'm quitting." He nodded again and headed for the front door.

When he heard the patter of slippered feet on the hardwood floor, he stopped. Sabine stood silhouetted in the dark hallway. She must have let him hear her follow.

"Jean-Luc," she said in a soft voice. "Thanks. For saving us."

"It wasn't me. It was you."

"You saved me and Meg and all of New Orleans. I just saved you," Sabine said lightly, as if it were nothing at all.

Jean-Luc huffed out a half-laugh and left, still not knowing where things stood between the two of them. Before he could ask, he had to do some soul-searching and come to terms with the choices he'd made, the things he'd done. After seeing him as a monster, Jean-Luc suspected Sabine needed space as well.

It's what they did, the two of them. They knocked heads, went their separate ways for a time, only to trip across one another's paths again. He didn't know if it would work out this time, not after he'd sunk so far, and she'd seen it all. Him in his own personal Hell. He didn't know if he was redeemable.

But the kiss—even if it were only to save his wretched hide—the kiss gave him hope.

Fool that he was.

Chapter 39

MEGAN

Meg barely noticed the chill in the visitors' room of the Orleans Parish Prison, not after her trip to the ice giants. Nothing on this side of the In Between could compare with the biting cold of the ice palace.

A buzzer sounded, and the door opened on the other side of the pane of bulletproof glass. Georgette came through looking bedraggled but smug. She sat leisurely in the chair across from Meg. They waited for the officer to leave before speaking.

Georgette lazily examined her pewter nails. The one on her pinky finger was missing, but the witch kept her hand curled so that it barely showed.

"What would you ask of Mlle. Georgette today, *Longues Jambes*?"

'Long Legs,' Meg had looked it up on an English to French app. She let the nickname slide off. She'd heard worse.

"No favors today, *La Chienne*." Meg had looked that one up, too. Georgette bristled. Maybe she wasn't faking her French accent. Meg smiled sweetly. "Instead, I brought you a gift, or rather, I'd like to return something stolen from you."

Wary but curious, Georgette leaned forward, ready to accept.

"You know I cannot pass it through the window. As before, I'll have my courier bring it to your cell."

Georgette leaned back, sullen. "That fox is a menace. If she stole something from Mlle. Georgette, how do you trust her to return it?"

"Trust me, Sabine does not want to keep it. Return to your cell, and I'll send it in." Meg stood to leave.

Georgette tapped a nail on the glass to get Meg's attention, leaving a knick in the smooth surface. "If the pup delivers it, why are you here?"

Meg let the sly smile she'd learned from the fae creep across her face. "Because I wanted you to know who it was from."

This time, Sabine waited obediently in the car. Meg got in, slammed the door, and tossed a silk bag into her lap. "Your turn."

Sabine hopped out of the car. "Don't bother waiting."

"I won't."

A moment later, a red fox darted across the parking lot. The silk bag dangled from its snout by a silver cord. The fox's black-tipped tail disappeared around the side of the Orleans Parish prison.

"It's a shame it's no longer white," Meg said to the crow peering in the window. "It was much easier to catch her sneaking around when it was white."

Bertrand bobbed his head in agreement.

Meg did wait, and listened until she was rewarded by the sound of Georgette wailing from behind the prison walls.

"Yeah, a broken heart hurts, doesn't it?" Meg pressed the heel of her hand against her sternum, where the steady ache remained, though the memory associated with it had been bartered away. "You'll get used to it."

She cranked up the reliable old Buick and headed for the Sassy Witch.

Chapter 40

───◆───

WARWICK

A moon's span had passed on this side of the In Between as Warwick wandered aimlessly through the human world. With his Writ of Business in hand, he could join the rebirth of the Faerie Market and rebuild his business.

But he did not.

He could chance returning to King Philip in hopes the boon of cleansing the market would earn him a place at court.

Yet he did not.

He considered briefly remaining in the witchling's shed with the faithful Bertand outside as a companion. A begrudging respect had blossomed for the petite thief. They might grow to be true allies, but what would be the fun in that?

So, he did not.

For a time, he rested in the arms of the ancient oaks scattered about the city like sentinels. He could commune with them longer, but he'd grown a restless spirit in his time with the humans.

Therefore, he did not.

And so the goblin found himself standing on the sidewalk outside a tourist shop in the heart of the French Quarter, contemplating whether or not to enter. The Sassy Witch had only just opened for the day and was most likely empty. But he hesitated.

Warwick had almost made up his mind to leave when a Creole man with a kind face and wise smile opened the door. He had a feeling of otherness about him, and Warwick wondered if the man were from the Beyond. No, the goblin wrote it off as simple homesickness.

The man tipped his hat as if in recognition and held the door open for Warwick. He spoke in a voice rich with the magic of sultry afternoons and lazy evenings. "She's waiting for you."

With that, Warwick stepped inside the Sassy Witch shop for the first time. A silver bell jingled over the door as it closed behind him. The clop of hooven feet drew him to the counter covered in lively crystals and pouches of Goofer Dust mixed with glitter, which gave off an oddly good humor.

"May I help you?" asked a young man with fawn-colored hair and cheerful brown eyes.

The glamour wrapping the satyr in a human form shimmered then solidified.

"I am here to ask for—"

"Warwick!" Megan Armand galloped from the back of the shop and threw her arms around him.

Warwick quelled the instinct to shrug her off, wrapped his arms around her, and patted her back as he'd seen elders do to excitable children.

"Are you back at Sabine's?" she asked as the satyr looked on, curious.

"Are you not?" he asked.

"Oh, so I guess you haven't spoken to her." Megan let go of him and took a step back, giving him space. "Before the, uhm, incident at the market, Georgette signed papers for me to take over the shop until she gets out. Which, considering how well she behaved last time, might be never. That includes her apartment. So, I packed up most of her things except the goth furniture, which suits the place, and moved in to run things."

"Ah, well," Warwick stammered, which was most unlike him.

"And you came looking for me," she grinned at the satyr as if to share this grand news with him. "Tohbi started this morning."

The satyr bowed low to the goblin. "I have heard so much about you."

"Ah, have you?" What had him at such a loss for words?

"If you're not staying at Sabine's, would you like to . . ." Megan waved a hand, gesturing to the shop. "Like to stay here? There's an enormous oak out back. It seems very stately."

"I'll consider the generous offer. But I came to ask for a," he hesitated, "a job. But I see you have a young helper. So, I'll be one my—Mph."

His words were cut off as his face collided with Megan's shoulder once more. She squealed in what he hoped was delight for a human, then held him at arm's length.

"Of course you can! Tohbi will read tarot. And I'll handle customers. And you . . . You'll grimace at sales reps who bring in cursed goods. Not that it'll happen often. They're mostly human and clueless, but they can be the worst kind." She laughed as if she'd made a joke.

The satyr smiled at her fondly.

And Warwick grimaced for practice and wondered what he had gotten himself into.

Chapter 41

THIBODEAUX

Jean-Luc balanced at the top of a ladder where he painted the second-story shutters of a white stucco building when he heard a familiar voice below, and his heart thudded in his chest.

"You know the entire police force is gonna make fun of you," Sabine said, examining a carved wooden plaque mounted beside the door below. It read, "Jean-Luc Thibodeaux, Private Detective, Specializing in the Paranormal and Supernatural."

"Yep. Most of them, but not all." He tried to quell the hope that rose in place of the black magic. The stain of the darkness remained, but its weight was gone. Mostly.

"I came by to see how you were holding up out here in the civilian world." She ran her hand along a crack in the stucco.

Jean-Luc cleaned the paint from his brush, closed the can, and climbed down. "I'm making it. Got two clients before I even had the sign up."

"Kooks?" Sabine tried the door, checking if it was locked. It wasn't, but she stayed outside.

He shrugged. "Who can tell?"

It was good just to see her. He'd stayed away, letting her decide if she wanted to have anything to do with him or not.

"Would you like to come in for a coffee, or something stronger?"

She peered through the windows that he'd just cleaned. "No. I have somewhere I need to be."

"Oh?" Jean-Luc raised a brow and shut down the disappointment. She'd come. It was a start.

"Some guy told me once that I needed training." She had yet to make eye contact.

"Wiseass."

She shrugged, looking down the block. Was she scared to be alone with him?

"The Voodoo priestesses going to help?"

"No, that's not their thing, but they introduced me to someone." He nodded, remembering, but she was looking at her shoes and didn't see it. "We'll see if she'll take me back. I didn't make the best first impression."

"Really?" he laughed, and Sabine flushed. "Don't worry. You charm us all in the end."

"You think?" She tipped her head up and met his eyes.

"I guarantee it." Jean-Luc's chest tightened. "Come see me when you're back in town. I might be looking for a partner."

She laughed. "Me get a legit job? Never."

"I didn't say anything about legit. Think about it," he said, as casually as he could, and returned to the ladder. No point in prolonging the goodbye.

Jean-Luc watched Sabine trail her fingers over the letters of his name as she walked away.

"Sabine," he called.

"Yeah?" she turned and looked up, her expression almost hopeful.

"Don't be gone too long, or I'll have to come hunting for you."

Sabine laughed, and his chest loosened. "Think you could find me?"

"Only if you wanted me to," he said with a smile and went back to painting. Once she turned away, Jean-Luc stopped to watch her go.

"I do," he thought he heard her say, but his hearing was probably as treacherous as his heart.

Chapter 42

❦

SABINE

Sabine circled the attic one last time. It had kept her safe for months when she first arrived in New Orleans and lived alone in the city. Jean-Luc was the only one who'd known where she'd hidden before meeting Meg. Well, he and Bertrand.

Later, she'd moved in with Meg while Jean-Luc quietly cleaned up her aunt's cottage. The stubborn detective had scrubbed blood from the floor, replaced cabinet doors scarred with bullet holes, and repainted the home in the same garish, eye-jarring colors that her aunt had chosen. Yet he still hadn't confessed to repairing the cottage, turning it into a home for her.

Meg had to point it out. Sabine had been unable or unwilling to believe it, lest it imparted her with some debt. Yet it had been obvious. Anyone could tell it by the way he knew where everything lived in the house—the cleaning supplies, the tools, the coffee filters. And she found herself surprisingly grateful, without the expected guilt.

Sabine hated leaving it. Before coming here, she'd coerced Meg into tending to the house, but she suspected her former housemate would put one of her new employees on it. After all, Meg had Georgette's shop to run. Sabine shuddered at the thought of Meg, or anyone sane, living in Georgette's apartment, but she suspected Meg had appetites that she wasn't interested in sharing.

A knock came at the window. The buzzard black crow tapped to get her attention. Sabine opened it, and Bertrand laid a fat, juicy caterpillar on the sill for her.

"*One for the road*," he *cackled*. "*But I see you've already packed.*" He hopped from the sill and landed beside her satchel. From there, he wedged himself under the eaves to peck at a second bag hidden in the shadows.

A worn black duffel bag was wedged into the space. In slightly darker black, where letters had been scraped from the canvas, you could read 'J. Thibodeaux'. Inside were cans of cold-brew cappuccino, dark chocolate energy bars, and mint Kit-Kats. He must have stashed it here for her before he found out Sabine had deserted the attic to move in with Meg.

She ducked her chin so Bertrand wouldn't see her smile and said, "Two out of three ain't bad. But, Lord, that man has a thing for mint chocolate. Maybe he's trying to indoctrinate me. We'll have to do something about that when we get back."

"*If,*" the bird *croaked*.

"Right. *If* we get back," she corrected. "It must have been here for months. You think it's still good?"

"Cruk."

"Yeah, well, you're a trash bird."

"*Cr-r-r-eek. What about me?*"

"Yes, I'm taking you, too. Consider it like pet obedience school but for familiars."

Bertrand *creaked* some more, then added, "*I fear there is no hope for your education. But I appreciate your willingness to learn.*"

Sabine hefted the duffel bag onto her shoulder and contemplated the satchel.

Bertrand *muttered*, "*Time to go. Time to go.*"

"Thank you. I don't need a ratty feather duster to tell me that." Sabine delicately lifted the satchel with the beaded necklace still hidden inside. With a resolute sigh, she pulled the strap over her head. The leather thrummed with energy, dark and sinister. "Let's go."

Bertrand *creaked* nervously.

"I know. I'm hiding them where no one can find them."

Carrying both the satchel and duffel bags, Sabine entered the forest in human form. Walking along the dirt trail, she adroitly stepped over cypress knees, letting the Spanish moss tickle her cheeks as she passed.

As the day gave way, she came to the edge of the bayou, where she set down the bags and transformed into a fox. Sitting back on her haunches, she waited.

The new moon set, leaving the waters lit only by starlight. Sabine's eyes sagged. She'd just drifted to sleep when a vibration jolted her awake. A worn wooden dock reached out from the floating island to the damp earth at her feet.

She stepped onto the weathered boards, and the island broke free. As she stepped foot onto the far side, she heard an old crone's cackle.

"Yeah. Yeah. We both knew I'd be back. You don't have to be smug about it."

Chapter 43

THIBODEAUX

Three Months Later

Carmichael walked into the corner coffee shop and queued up behind Jean-Luc. He stepped to the side so she could read the menu and to keep her in his line of sight. If you'd asked him six months ago if he trusted her, he'd have said absolutely, but a lot had happened in those six months.

"You're out awfully early," Carmichael said as she studied the chalkboard over the barista's head. "Being your own boss, you'd think you'd cut yourself some slack."

Jean-Luc gave a half laugh, its edge so bitter he could taste it. The young, freckled cashier asked for their orders. Carmichael waved for him to go ahead.

"Medium coffee, black," Jean-Luc said.

"That's awfully boring," Carmichael chided.

While she ordered, he accepted the cup and left.

"Jean-Luc," Carmichael called. "Hold up a minute."

Shit.

Jean-Luc stopped just outside the closed door. As he waited, he searched the early morning fog for peculiarities—clopping feet, slithering corpses, shrieks of terror. It took Carmichael a while to join him, and Jean-Luc couldn't help but think it was a power-play. Damn, he had become suspicious. She came out carrying a bag of pastries and a fancy mixed coffee and jerked her head towards the table. "Let's have a seat."

Reluctantly, he sat down, angling himself toward the street, while she faced him full on.

"What you got?" Jean-Luc asked.

"Ease up a minute." Taking out a blueberry muffin, Carmichael set it on a plate and slid it towards him, then took out another for herself. She leaned back and took a slow drink of coffee, mimed scalding her tongue, and set it down to cool as if they had all the time in the world to visit. He didn't.

Jean-Luc had a city to protect, whether he had a badge on or not. He gestured for her to talk.

"You're missed back at the precinct," Carmichael said, nibbling at her muffin and nodding for him to start his, as if he were a child who needed encouragement.

Jean-Luc remained calm and didn't respond. The darkness rose when his anger did. It had been three months since the purging of the Faerie Market. Since Sabine stole the darkness from him. But he lived in fear that it might return, and she might not.

There was nothing to say to Carmichael at any rate. His days as a detective with the NOPD were over. He could not keep the city safe within the confines of their limited human viewpoint. He took a drink of coffee and surveilled the mists. She had one more minute to get to the point. Carmichael sipped her coffee, looking agitated that he had yet to touch her offering.

In the street, a silhouette darted through the mists, low to the ground, moving fast and silent. The only evidence of its passing was the vortex of fog left behind. Jean-Luc finished his coffee in one swallow and motioned for the server. "One medium latte, lots of foam, add a squirt of hazelnut, and a croissant."

Rallying, Carmichael smirked. "A fancy coffee but no blueberry muffin? Or is the drink for me?" she asked as if she were creating a dossier on him.

"To go," he added to the server, which irritated Carmichael. "You have until he returns to tell me why you're here."

Suddenly serious, Carmichael leaned over the table. "That pet thief of yours. Where is she?"

"Who can say?" Jean-Luc kept his eyes trained on his former assistant.

"*I* need to know." She sounded desperate.

"Sorry. Can't help you. I'm just a civilian." He stood to pay the server and take the bag and coffee.

Carmichael reached for his arm. "She's trouble. If you see her or hear from her, call me immediately. And stay clear. I'm telling you this as a friend, Jean-Luc."

"That's Mr. Thibodeaux to you," he said, dislodging her hand, and stepped into the fog.

Carmichael hissed. Jean-Luc could tell something had her scared.

The fog muted the streetlamps and muffled all sound but Jean-Luc's footsteps. It only took half a block before Carmichael and the shop disappeared from view. He rolled his shoulders and popped his neck.

"Come out of the shadows before your coffee gets cold and I decide to eat your croissant."

The patter of padded feet quickened and was replaced by the whisper-soft shushing of slippers on the sidewalk as a woman in an auburn jumper fell into step beside him.

"You should have gotten two," Sabine said. "The first one only makes me hungry." Without looking his way, she held out a hand for the latte. He handed it over and placed the bag in her other hand.

They walked, neither of them touching, his arm only a hair's breadth away from hers. Tension flowed from his muscles as Jean-Luc relaxed for the first time since he'd caught the petite thief tumbling out of a window last fall. Sabine was back, and she was safe. He would make sure of that.

They continued in companionable silence for another block before she asked, "So, about that partnership?"

Author's Note

Thanks for joining me in the Big Easy!

A Clever Fox wraps up the first trilogy of the *Faerie Market Mysteries*. I hope you enjoyed visiting the sultry city of New Orleans, teaming with people from all over this world and the Beyond.

For the free prequel, join my newsletter, DREAMARC.
https://subscribepage.io/JuliaVAshley-Newsletter

There, you will be notified when the next trilogy releases and receive news on upcoming stories of hidden magic, centuries-old buildings, and scrappy characters, as well as, news about sales and free short fiction.

Until then . . .
Soignez vous-autres!

About the Author

Julia V. Ashley writes paranormal mysteries and contemporary fantasy, including the Faerie Market Mysteries Books One & Two (*A Charmed Moon* and *An Enchanted Heart*), *Jazz by Faelight: Original Short Stories of Hidden Magic in the Big Easy*, and "No Nibbling on the Neighbors," originally published in the *Vampire Survival Guide*.

As an architect, Julia finds inspiration delving into the crumbling buildings of the Gothic South where she grew up. She lives along the Natchez Trace Parkway with her husband, surrounded by a menagerie of wildlife roaming the woods.

For more info visit:
https://juliavashley.com/